ROOFTOP WAR ZONE!

"Get out of here, Spider-Man!" said the Hulk. "The fire can't harm me, but you don't have any kind of protection."

"Nothing doing, Doc!" replied Spidey. "I've got a reputation to uphold, you know! Besides, I think Round Two's about to start!"

Through the heart of the blaze walked the Super-Skrull. The hatred in his eyes burned as brightly as the flames around him.

The Super-Skrull gnashed his teeth and growled. His eyes seemed to glow with an unnatural light as he glared at the web-spinner.

And then something unseen smashed into Spidey's head with the speed of a bullet train. He staggered to the edge of the roof.

"Spider-Man!" cried the Hulk. The jade giant spun quickly, trying to grab hold of the wall-crawler, but it was too late.

Spider-Man toppled over the side.

SPIDER-MAN
SUPER THRILLER
— WARRIOR'S REVENGE —

SPIDER-MAN®

SUPER THRILLER

— WARRIOR'S REVENGE —

Neal Barrett, Jr.
Illustrations by James W. Fry

BYRON PREISS MULTIMEDIA COMPANY, INC.

NEW YORK

POCKET BOOKS
NEW YORK   LONDON   TORONTO   SYDNEY   TOKYO   SINGAPORE

An *Original* Publication of POCKET BOOKS

POCKET BOOKS, a division of Simon & Schuster Inc.
1230 Avenue of the Americas, New York, NY 10020

Copyright © 1997 Marvel Characters, Inc.
A Byron Preiss Multimedia Company, Inc. Book

Byron Preiss Multimedia Company, Inc.
24 West 25th Street
New York, New York 10010

The Byron Preiss Multimedia Worldwide Web Site Address is:
http://www.byronpreiss.com

ISBN 0-671-00800-5

First Pocket Books paperback printing August 1997

10 9 8 7 6 5 4 3 2 1

Edited by Steve Roman
Cover art by Mike Zeck and Phil Zimelman
Cover design by Claude Goodwin
Interior design by MM Design 2000, Inc.

Printed in the U.S.A.

CHAPTER
1

"Stampede" wasn't the first word that came to Spider-Man's mind as he swung above the neon-lit streets of the New York City area called Times Square. It was "panic."

On a normal evening, Times Square is the center of entertainment in the Big Apple. Its streets are lined with shops, restaurants, theatres and movie houses; its sidewalks are tightly packed with visitors and tourists from around the world. But it was a sure bet that the city's tourist board didn't have in mind what was happening this night.

Spider-Man looked down on a scene of pure chaos. Horns blared. Sirens wailed. Cars collided, and people screamed in terror as they ran in all directions. Traffic was backed up along both Broadway and Seventh Avenue as far as the eye could see. The congestion spilled out through the sidestreets that intersected the area, creating a jam of monstrous proportions. Parents clutched their children tightly as the panicked crowd began to trample each other in their haste to get away. Police officers swarmed through the streets, trying desperately to restore order.

And standing in the center of all this was a seven-foot-tall, green-skinned giant who went by the name of Dr. Robert Bruce Banner.

Most people, though, knew him only as the incredible Hulk.

"Come back here, coward!" bellowed the Hulk. His shout rattled windows in buildings several blocks away. "I haven't pounded on you half as much as I plan to!" He charged through the intersection, tossing aside any vehicle that blocked his path.

Perched atop a billboard advertising the latest Sega video game, his internal warning system—his spider-sense—screaming *danger!*, Spider-Man tried to make sense of the scene below.

I don't get it, he thought. *The Hulk hasn't gone on one of his mindless rampages in months, not since Doc Banner found a way to keep his intelligent mind in control of the Hulk's body. So why is he acting so crazed? Who could he be chasing? Must be someone pretty powerful, if he's this riled.*

Swinging down for a closer look, Spider-Man gazed in the direction the Hulk was heading . . . and couldn't believe what he saw.

Running up the middle of Broadway, thirty yards ahead of the Hulk, was an old man. Legs pumping frantically, the man—who seemed to be well into his seventies—weaved in and out of the congested traffic, his thin arms wrapped protectively around a large metal suitcase.

"Come back and face me!" the Hulk roared. Using

"Come back here, coward!" bellowed the Hulk. "I haven't pounded on you half as much as I plan to!"

his powerful leg muscles, he launched himself into the air, attempting to close the distance between him and the old man. Air whistled past the jade giant as he flew, missile-like, straight at the senior citizen. The man turned to look back, his eyes widening in shock as he saw the green behemoth flying at him. There appeared to be no escape . . .

. . . Until Spider-Man swooped down, grabbed the old man around the waist, and swung them both out of the Hulk's path.

The Hulk landed with a loud *thoom!* that cracked the pavement, tossed cars on their sides, shattered windows, and knocked people off their feet. The green-skinned scientist looked around at the destruction he'd just caused and frowned.

"Sorry," he said, sheepishly, to the bystanders struggling to their feet. "I *did* promise my wife I wouldn't go jumping around like that. Guess I got carried away." Brushing dust out of his dark green hair, the Hulk watched as Spider-Man swung up Broadway, the old man safely tucked under one arm.

"Spider-Man," groaned the Hulk. "That just tops off the day I've been having." Sighing heavily, he set off after the pair.

A half-mile away, Spidey checked to make sure the Hulk wasn't close enough to see them. Then he made a quick turn around the corner of West Fifty-sixth Street, landed on the sidewalk, and gently put the old man down. The senior smoothed out the oversized Hawaiian shirt that hung loosely off his scarecrow-like frame. He still clung tightly to his suitcase.

"Sorry for the rough ride, sir," Spidey said, "but under the circumstances . . ."

"That's quite all right," said the man, brushing back his thinning white hair with a gnarled hand. "Especially when it was a choice between a bumpy trip and that brute landing on me."

"Yes, about that," said Spidey. "You wanna clue me in as to why ol' Greenskin's after you, Mr. . . . ?"

"Mantlo," said the man. "And I haven't the slightest idea. There I was, minding my own business—I'm the type of person who believes in minding his own business, you understand—when that . . . creature started screaming at me. Before I knew it, I was running for my life!"

"It wouldn't have anything to do with that suitcase, would it?" asked Spidey, eyeing the sophisticated design of the metal casing. *It sure doesn't look like something this guy would normally carry around,* he thought.

"No, it does not!" asserted Mantlo. He gripped the case even tighter, glaring angrily at the web-slinger. "Are you calling me a *thief?!*"

For the first time, Spidey noticed the crowd of onlookers that had been watching them. They moved in closer at the old man's cry of outrage, some of the burlier men in the crowd appearing ready to attack the wall-crawler.

Uh-oh, thought Spidey as the crowd formed a rough, tight semicircle around him. *Nice to see I'm as popular as always with the general public. This is gonna get really ugly unless I cool off this situation right away.*

"No, sir, I'm not," assured Spidey, hands held open in a non-threatening manner toward Mantlo. "I'm just looking for a reason as to why the Hulk would go flying off the handle like this."

"Oh," said Mantlo. He paused a moment, then nodded his head, as if in agreement. "Then I apologize for my misunderstanding."

From the corner of his eye, Spidey saw the crowd relax and move back a step. *One crisis averted,* he thought with relief.

"I wish I could help you, Spider-Man," said the old man, "but I can't. I was just minding my own business, after all." He smiled, looking warm and friendly and vulnerable.

But if this guy is so friendly, thought Spidey, *why hasn't my spider-sense eased up since I first saw him running from the Hulk?* He frowned. *There's more to this guy than he's letting on.*

"Well," said Mantlo, taking a step back, "I really must be going."

Turning to leave, Mantlo stumbled as his heel caught on a crack in the pavement. His grip on the suitcase loosened as he fought to keep his balance, and the metal valise struck the sidewalk. A trio of bystanders caught the old man before he hit the ground, while Spider-Man bent down and picked up the case.

"Hey," he commented, "this thing's pretty heavy. You need a hand carrying this?"

"NO!" shouted Mantlo, snatching the valise back. "I don't need anybody's help!" He clutched the case tightly. "Besides," he added, "I'm stronger than I look."

"My mistake," said Spidey.

"Stop him!" roared a voice from behind, interrupting Spidey's thoughts. The web-slinger turned around to look down Broadway. It was the voice of the Hulk, who was closing fast.

"Persistent little devil, isn't he?" Spidey said as he watched the Hulk clearing a path up the avenue. He turned back to face Mantlo. "If I get him to calm down, would you—?"

The old man had wasted no time in taking flight again. Spidey caught sight of the gaudy Hawaiian shirt as it turned the corner on Eighth Avenue, heading northwest toward Fifty-seventh Street.

"Perfect," muttered Spidey. "Just perfect." He sighed, then turned back to face the charging Hulk. The giant's booted footfalls sent tremors through the pavement.

"Get out of my way, Spider-Man!" ordered the Hulk as he drew near. "You're not going to protect that killer any longer!"

"Hold on a minute, Doc." Spidey held up his hands, signalling the Hulk to stop. "What killer—that old man? If he's a killer, then I'm—"

"A minor obstacle," remarked the Hulk. Without breaking stride, he gripped the front of Spidey's costume in one gigantic hand and tossed the web-slinger high into the air. The crowd of on-lookers scattered as the Hulk continued on his way, heading for Fifty-seventh Street.

Twenty stories above Broadway, Spider-Man's unplanned trip came to an abrupt ending with a rough landing on the roof of an office building.

"Oww," moaned Spidey, rubbing his sore back. "He could've at least provided some complimentary peanuts for that flight."

Slowly rising to his feet, Spidey peered over the edge of the roof. Down on Fifty-sixth Street, the Hulk was just turning the corner onto Eighth Avenue. Triggering his web-shooters, Spidey shot a line at the cornice of an adjoining building, then sadly shook his head.

"Going toe-to-toe with the Hulk," he muttered. "I oughtta have my head examined." Leaping from the roof, Spidey twisted his body so that the arc of his swing carried him around the corner in pursuit of the Hulk.

On the corner of Eighth Avenue and Fifty-seventh Street, the Hulk came to a halt and gazed around the intersection. There was no sign of the old man. The jade giant growled softly, startling a group of dogs being walked by a mousy-looking woman in her thirties. Amid a chorus of yelps and barks, the animals ran for the protection of the opposite side of the street, dragging the poor woman behind them. The Hulk sighed.

"Having a bad day, Doc?" said a voice from above. The Hulk glanced up to find Spider-Man hanging upside-down from a web attached to the top of a nearby lamp post.

"Don't you have a fly to catch or something?" asked the Hulk, clearly annoyed. "I think you've caused enough trouble for one day."

"Well, I am *terribly* sorry for spoiling your fun, Doc," said Spidey, sarcastically. "What happened—the Fantastic Four is out of town this week, so you thought you'd kill some time by chasing around senior citizens?"

The Hulk glared angrily at Spidey, his massive green hands clenching into fists. It was obvious he was fighting to remain calm.

"You just don't get it, do you?" the Hulk said, pointing an accusing finger at Spidey. "That was no old man you helped escape—it was the Super-Skrull!"

CHAPTER
2

Mantlo was no longer an old man. Walking casually away from Eighth Avenue, he had transformed himself into a dirt-covered vagrant, dressed in tattered jeans and T-shirt and moth-eaten overcoat. It was the perfect disguise for use in escaping the Hulk's wrath since—as Skrull spies on Earth had discovered long ago—homeless people were generally ignored by the populace. It was the closest thing to being invisible.

Reaching the corner of Fifty-seventh Street and Ninth Avenue, the "vagrant" turned into a teenage boy on rollerblades, and whipped through the freely-flowing traffic headed south. He shifted his shape whenever he changed streets, moving swiftly away from midtown.

K'lrt, the Super-Skrull, was angry. He hated the humans, hated the distasteful forms he was forced to assume in order to move freely among them. He hated having to hide his true appearance, his true nature as a proud warrior of the Skrull Empire.

But most of all, he hated the *superpowered* humans. Spider-Man. The Hulk. The Fantastic Four. The Avengers. Miserable Earth creatures gifted with powers far beyond those of their fellow humans. But did they put these powers to any good use, such as taking control of this planet and ruling it like gods? No. They preferred dressing in gaudy costumes that hid their identities, and used their abilities to help nonpowered humans who were obviously inferior to them.

It seemed that, everywhere K'lrt turned, there stood one or another of these colorfully garbed "super heroes"— as they were called by the planet's news gathering media—performing some act of *kindness*. How pathetic! And some of these heroes were actually females. K'lrt sneered in disgust. Women! Fighting battles that were best left to men.

K'lrt shook his head. He would never understand these creatures. The whole planet needed to be fumigated, purified, wiped clean of the human vermin. The Empire would not rest until this task was completed. *That* would be a day to truly stir the blood of every Skrull in the distant galaxy of Andromeda.

Before that day could come, though, he had a mission to carry out—one that the Hulk had kept him from completing. K'lrt gnashed his teeth. He was frustrated by the continual interference of these costumed heroes; they were as numerous as flies in this stifling city . . . and even more annoying. But soon enough, the Hulk would learn the price of crossing paths with the Super-Skrull . . .

*   *   *

When Spider-Man's alter-ego, Peter Parker, awoke that morning, he'd felt like all was right in the world. Of course, being Spider-Man, that feeling wasn't going to last long.

After a week of tracking down the Vulture—one of his oldest, deadliest foes—Spidey had finally cornered the winged felon at a Queens construction site and, after a spectacular battle, had defeated his enemy and delivered him to the police. Best of all, Spidey's automatic camera had worked without a hitch, so he had photographs of the fight to sell to the *Daily Bugle*.

And selling pictures meant that Peter and his wife, Mary Jane, would be able to tackle the mountain of bills they faced—a pile that never seemed to grow smaller. At the moment, MJ was waiting for news from the producers of the action movie *Fatal Action III* as to whether there was to be a fourth film in the series. MJ had co-starred in *Fatal Action III*, playing a police detective fighting terrorists in New York. But until the next movie got the go-ahead, MJ had no job, which left Peter as the only moneymaker in the family.

After developing the Vulture photographs in his darkroom, Peter headed for the *Bugle*. Unfortunately, the first person he ran into there was *Bugle* publisher J. Jonah Jameson, a man known for two distinctive characteristics: a really bad haircut and a hair-trigger temper.

Jonah had wasted no time in corraling Peter into another assignment. However, Jonah was not looking to help Peter pay his bills, or to reward him for the exclusive photos of Spider-Man defeating the Vulture.

Peter was just the first photographer Jonah laid eyes on that day.

A banquet and awards ceremony was being held by the Partnership for Humanity, which was a human rights organization dedicated to freeing political prisoners around the world. The festivities—held at the Platinum Towers Hotel—were in honor of world-famous science-fiction writer Berkley Whitmore, the author of more than one hundred novels over the course of thirty years. But Whitmore did more than just write books. He was also an outspoken supporter of the Partnership. He lectured on its goals. He spoke about the evils of oppressive governments. He traveled around the country and around the world in support of the Partnership.

Shoving his freelance photographer toward the bank of elevators outside the newsroom, Jonah had explained that Joy Mercado—one of the *Bugle*'s ace reporters—would be waiting for Peter in the lobby of the Platinum Towers. Since it was a formal occasion, Jonah told Peter to rent a tuxedo, or at least "wear something halfway decent." Peter had returned home, pulled his best suit out of mothballs and, as night fell, headed off to meet Joy.

But before he had reached the hotel, the Hulk started turning Times Square into a war zone and, of course, Peter had to find out what was going on. He'd quickly found a place to change from his dress clothes into his Spidey-suit. Webbing the clothes together in a tight bundle, he'd left them on a rooftop in Times Square. Peter had hoped to pick them up again in time to meet Joy at the awards ceremony.

But now Peter would miss the banquet. He could

only hope his suit would still be webbed to the rooftop whenever he could get back to it.

The old Spidey luck was running true to form . . .

"Explain to me again why we're not chasing down the Super-Skrull, Doc," said Spider-Man, swinging from lampposts as the Hulk walked down Broadway.

"*I'm* not going after him because I have something more important to do," replied the Hulk. "My wife, Betty, was with me when the Skrull attacked, and I had to leave her behind to chase him. I want to make sure she's all right." He waved a hand at Spidey in a dismissive gesture. "There's nothing stopping *you* from looking for him, though. *You're* the super hero."

"Well, to be honest with you, Doc," said Spidey, hesitantly, "the Super-Skrull's a little out of my league. I'd appreciate a helping hand."

The Hulk grunted. "Oh, all right. But Betty comes first."

Spidey nodded in agreement. Had their positions been reversed, and Mary Jane had been the one facing possible injury, Spidey's thoughts would have been focused on his wife, as well.

"Lovely night for a stroll, isn't it?" asked Spidey after a few moments.

The Hulk looked up at Spidey as though he had three heads.

"Do these little quips come to you naturally," the green-skinned scientist asked sarcastically, "or do you actually pay somebody to write them for you?"

"Sheesh!" said Spidey. "A guy tries to lighten up a situation and what does he get for his troubles? Insults!" He tugged at the front of his costume as though he were wearing a tie. "I tell ya, Doc—I don't get no respect!"

"I see," replied the Hulk, nodding his head knowingly. "You don't have to pay for your jokes. You steal them from Rodney Dangerfield."

They were back at Times Square, which was in the same mess it had been a half-hour earlier. Streets were still congested like hamburger fat clogging a heart's arteries, and it would take hours before any normal flow of traffic could be restored. The Hulk's antics during the height of rush hour had quickly established him as the Most Hated Superbeing in New York. The jeers and boos from hostile bystanders was proof of that.

"So, what was this all about, Doc?" asked Spidey. "When the Super-Skrull drops by the Big Apple, he's usually looking to pick a fight with the Avengers or the Fantastic Four. How'd he happen to run into you?"

"Bad timing," replied the Hulk, "on *his* part. Betty and I were attending an awards dinner at the Platinum Towers Hotel and—"

"The one honoring Berkley Whitmore?" said Spidey. The Hulk, surprised, looked at him. "You know about that?"

"Uh, yeah," said Spidey, fumbling for an explanation that wouldn't give away his secret identity. "I . . . heard about it on the news. I've been a fan of Whitmore's work ever since high school. I think it's great that he's being honored like this."

The Hulk smiled. "Do you want me to introduce you to him?"

Behind his mask, Spidey's eyes widened in surprise. "You know Berkley Whitmore?"

"Sure," said the Hulk. "Berk and I are long-time friends, but I hadn't seen him in years." He frowned. "Being constantly hounded by the military and every super-villain and super hero in creation"—he looked up at Spidey—"makes it hard to keep friends. That's why Betty and I were here tonight—I wanted to get together with Berk, talk about old times. But when the Skrull showed up and tried to kill him . . ."

"*What?*" exclaimed Spidey. "Why would the Super-Skrull want to kill a science-fiction writer?"

Reaching the corner of Forty-sixth Street and Broadway, the Hulk turned left to head East toward Sixth Avenue. Spidey continued to keep pace with him.

"I'm still trying to figure that out," the Hulk replied. "On the surface, it doesn't make any sense. Then again, Skrulls aren't exactly known for cluing everyone in on their plans." He shrugged. "Hopefully, Berk will have some idea of what this is about." He gestured in the direction they were traveling. "We're here."

Spidey looked down the street. Ahead of them was the Platinum Towers Hotel, and it was immediately obvious that the Hulk's pursuit of the Super-Skrull had begun here. A gaping, ragged hole in one wall was evidence that at least one of the combatants hadn't bothered to exit through the building's door. A delivery van lay on its side near the hotel's side entrance, its chassis crumpled like the bellows of an accordion. A pair of oversized hand prints could be seen pressed into the metal. Strewn down the length of the block were a number of other vehicles, equally damaged.

In addition to the wrecks, the street was now filled with police cars, fire trucks, and ambulances. As firemen streamed inside to check the building's wiring system—which may have been damaged by the fight—the police had cordoned off the street to keep back curious passersby and members of the press. Hotel guests had been evacuated in case the fight had caused structural damage.

The Hulk pointed to the wrecks. "Just as I was closing in on him, he started tossing parked cars to try to slow me down. It worked, too. I spent so much time trying to protect bystanders that he got a good head-start down the street. Then he shapeshifted into the form of that old man."

Under his mask, Spidey's face flushed red with embarrassment. "Uh, yeah. Again, I'm really sorry for butting in like that, Doc. But you *know* what it looked like . . ."

The Hulk nodded. "I understand, Spider-Man. You don't need to apologize." He smiled. "Besides, based on the way I used to act, mindlessly smashing everything in sight, *I* would have thought I was on a rampage."

Spidey's gaze drifted to the smashed vehicles. "I don't get it," he said. "Why didn't he just use his powers? After all, the Skrull has the combined abilities of the Fantastic Four."

The Hulk rubbed his jaw. "I don't know. It also doesn't make sense that he'd run from a fight. He's always prided himself with being a 'mighty warrior'."

"We're curious about that, too," said a voice behind them. Spidey and the Hulk turned around.

Standing beside a sleek, car-sized hovercraft was a tall African-American woman wearing a black leather uniform—one instantly recognizable to both heroes.

"SAFE," growled the Hulk. "Just perfect."

SAFE—an acronym for Strategic Action For Emergencies—was an organization created "to handle paranormal and domestic crises that are beyond the capabilities of traditional law-enforcement agencies," as its charter stated. In simpler terms, it meant that the group worked on unusual cases—usually involving superbeings—that threatened the security of the United States of America. SAFE answered directly to the president. On one particular mission, Spider-Man and the Hulk had worked with SAFE agents to put a stop to the plans of two villainous organizations, Hydra and AIM.

Working with a government agency in the past, however, didn't mean the Hulk tolerated their arrival on the scene now.

Ignoring the Hulk's sneer, Spider-Man extended a hand to the woman. "Major . . . Jones, isn't it?"

"That's right," replied the woman, shaking his hand. "Major Nefertiti Jones. Good to see you again, Spider-Man."

"I wish it was under better circumstances," said Spidey.

Jones smiled wistfully. "People like us only seem to meet under circumstances like this."

"Unfortunately," agreed Spidey.

Spidey looked around at the scene of chaos that swirled around them. Police officials were conferring with fire chiefs. SAFE agents swept across the area's perimeters, watchful for any action that could be considered a threat to them. Spidey's gaze locked on a group of reporters pressing against the police barricades.

At the front of the pack was Joy Mercado, the *Daily*

Bugle reporter Peter Parker was supposed to meet for the awards dinner. A stunningly beautiful blond, Joy—dressed in a black evening gown, her long hair piled stylishly atop her head—looked out of place among the rumpled suits, weathered polyester slacks, and scuffed shoes of some of her male colleagues. Behind his mask, Spidey chewed on his bottom lip as he watched Joy try to bully a weary police officer into letting her past the barricade.

So, what am I gonna tell Joy this time? the wall-crawler wondered. *I've given her so many excuses in the past for missing appointments that I'm starting to forget which ones I've told her.*

"Look," interjected the Hulk, stepping between Spidey and Jones, "if we're all through getting reacquainted, I've got a wife to check on." He turned to Jones. "You wouldn't happen to know where she is, would you?"

"Of course, Doctor Banner," replied Jones. "Right this way." She led the heroes to an armor-plated troop transport ringed by a squad of SAFE agents.

The Hulk lumbered toward the van. Before he could reach it, though, a youthful-looking agent stepped forward to block his path.

"One moment, sir," said the agent. He reached to his belt for an instrument the size of a handheld calculator.

The Hulk warily eyed the instrument. "Explain what that is *now* before you wind up explaining to a doctor how it got wedged in your throat."

The agent coolly ignored the threat. "Bio-scan. This'll just take a second, Doctor." Activating the device, he pointed it at the Hulk, then watched the read-

ings displayed on a small screen. He nodded to the
jade giant. "All done."

Jones stepped forward so the same procedure could
be run on her. She turned to the Hulk. "Since Skrulls
can make themselves look like anyone, we asked Reed
Richards of the Fantastic Four to come up with something we could use to detect disguised aliens."

"You thought I might be the Super-Skrull?" growled
the Hulk.

"Let me put it to you this way, Doctor: With the
Super-Skrull on the loose, would you want us to put
your wife and Mr. Whitmore at risk by *not* making
sure of your identity?"

The Hulk shook his head. "No."

"We know our jobs, Doctor Banner," said Jones.
"Our procedures might be a pain in the neck sometimes, but they've kept us alive this long." She turned
to Spidey. "Spider-Man, you're next."

The agent conducted his scan of Spidey, checked the
results, and nodded his head. "Everyone checks out.
We're good to go."

"All right," said Jones. "Then, let's check on your
wife, Doc—"

The transport's door flew open with a loud *clang!*
SAFE agents whirled around quickly, weapons drawn.

"Hey!" barked a sharp, slightly nasal voice. "How
long do you *yutzes* plan on keeping me cooped up in
this sardine can?"

Berkley Whitmore ambled out of the transport. He
walked with a gangling, lazy motion, as if his arms
and legs somehow might be attached with hinges. His
hair was a mass of wild strands the color of copper
wire. His nose showed signs of having been broken in

19

the middle a long time ago, and his cobalt-blue eyes were hooded under heavy lids. To Spidey, he looked like a man ready to lie down and take a nap.

Still, Spider-Man knew there was a razor-edged mind beneath that explosion of hair. Whitmore turned out more fiction than any five writers put together, and everything he wrote was strange, shocking, brilliant or downright disgusting, depending on who you talked to. Everybody had an opinion about his work. No one was undecided about Berkley Whitmore.

Whitmore frowned at the agents. "Huh! Critics everywhere! Is this how you usually treat great intellectuals," he asked, staring at the guns trained on him, "or do all of you have a problem with my writing?"

"Everyone stand down!" ordered Jones. The agents holstered their weapons. Jones stepped forward to join Whitmore. "Sorry about that, Mr. Whitmore. We're all on edge a bit."

Whitmore's eyes flared with anger. "Being on edge, Major, does not give your men the right to draw weapons on an unarmed civilian. That's the kind of militaristic mentality I've been fighting against since before you were born." He thrust out his chin, using it to point at the SAFE agents. "Your men would do well to consider the consequences of their actions before some innocent bystander gets hurt."

"I'll keep that in mind," replied Jones, huffily.

Spidey edged over to the Hulk. "I thought the stories I'd heard about the way he rips into people were exaggerated, but now . . ." He nodded toward Whitmore. "Has he always been like that?"

"For as long as I've known him," said the Hulk. "And Berk hasn't even warmed up yet." He lumbered

"Is this how you usually treat great intellectuals," Whitmore asked, "or do all of you have a problem with my writing?"

forward. "Come on. I want to find out where Betty is." SAFE agents parted like the Red Sea as the heroes headed for the transport.

As the Hulk approached, the anger faded from Whitmore's eyes, replaced by a mirthful sparkle. The author smiled broadly.

"Bruce!" he yelled. "Back from your jog around the block? I hear you've become very popular with the Department of Traffic after your little adventure over on Broadway."

"Well, you know how I am about party-crashers," said the Hulk. "Especially when they start shooting at my friends."

"A trait of yours for which I'll be eternally grateful," said Whitmore. He looked around the Hulk's massive frame. "Who's your colorful friend?"

"Oops!" said the Hulk. "Sorry about that." He gestured toward Spidey. "Berkley Whitmore, I'd like you to meet Spider-Man."

"Ah," said Whitmore. "The fashion victim." He flashed a half-smile at Spidey. "I've heard a lot of stories about you, Spider-Man. They usually involve you punching Bruce in the face and him trying to drop a building or two on your head."

"Yeah," Spidey said, sarcastically. "Those were the days." He stepped forward to shake Whitmore's hand—

—and froze, as his spider-sense warned him of nearby danger!

CHAPTER

— 3 —

It was just a mild tingle from his spider-sense, like an itch at the base of his skull. Still, Spider-Man knew that it wouldn't have kicked in unless something was wrong. He looked around at the assemblage of cops, firemen, and government agents, then turned to scan the throngs of bystanders crowded against the police barricades at the ends of the block.

Whitmore, his hand still outstretched, raised a quizzical eyebrow as he watched Spider-Man's curious behavior. Lowering his hand, Whitmore turned to the Hulk.

"Is your friend just preoccupied," Whitmore asked, "or is he always this rude?"

"What's wrong, Berk?" replied the Hulk. "Don't like being beaten at your own game?"

"*Hmmf!*" huffed Whitmore. Frowning at the Hulk, he folded his arms across his chest and said nothing.

Spider-Man walked a few paces away from the armor-plated van and stared at the crowd. The buzzing was still there in his head—not weak, not strong, just . . . there.

Could the Super-Skrull have doubled back? Spider-Man thought. *He could be hiding anywhere.*

"Something troubling you, Spider-Man?" asked Nefertiti Jones, sidling close to the web-slinger to keep her voice low.

"Maybe," Spidey said slowly. "Major, I'm pretty sure you can vouch for your men, that none of them is the Super-Skrull. But since he got away from Doc Banner and me, is it possible he could—"

"Be hiding among the crowd?" Jones said, completing his question. From the look on her face, it was clear she was mentally kicking herself. She turned to the youthful agent with the bio-scanner. "Elfman!"

Elfman trotted over, his closely-cropped brown hair waving in the slight breeze like rows of wheat. "Yes, ma'am?"

Jones gestured toward the crowd. "Take your team and hit both ends of this street. I want a wide-range scan of all these people."

Elfman's eyes widened, his skin turning a sickly gray. "*All* of them, ma'am?"

"You heard me, mister!" barked Jones. "We've got a potential Level Three situation here!"

"Right away, ma'am!" responded Elfman. He hurried off to assemble the other agents who carried similar bio-scanners.

Spider-Man watched the SAFE agents spread out, then turned to Jones. "A 'Level Three situation'?" he asked.

Jones showed a brief half-smile. "Would you rather I blurted out we're looking for a Skrull?"

Spidey nodded his head. "Ah! Point taken."

Whitmore strode over to join them, the Hulk in tow.

"Where are your bully-boys off to, Major?" asked Whitmore. "Some jaywalker need to be taught a lesson?"

Jones sighed. "No, Mr. Whitmore. We're just running a security sweep of the area."

"Why?" said Whitmore. "You think that bat-eared thug might be around here?" He caught the look of surprise that passed between Spidey and Jones. "Oh, come on, people!" he yelled. "I didn't just fall off the turnip truck! The guy is a Skrull and, if my knowledge of that race is accurate, he has the ability to look like any average *schmoe* in that staring, vacant-eyed mob out there!"

"Wait a minute. How do you know Skrulls have that power?" Spidey asked.

Whitmore glared at him like he was talking to an idiot. "Hey, pal, you think that after thirty years of writing science-fiction stories, I'm not familiar with the concept of shapeshifting? Besides, Betty told me all about the time she and Bruce ran into the Super-Skrull in some little backwater town in Utah."

"Bunkport," said a voice behind them. Recognizing it, the Hulk turned around, a wide smile coming instantly to his lips.

"Betty!" he exclaimed.

Elizabeth Banner stepped from the transport, dressed in jeans, hiking boots, and black T-shirt. A slight breeze ruffled shoulder-length red hair—her choice of hair color for that week. Not the type to wear jewelry, Betty still managed to draw attention to herself by her unusual choice of clothing accessory: a weather-beaten, leather shoulder harness housing a SAFE-issue laser pistol. Observing this combination of good looks and lethal weaponry, Spidey thought of actress Linda Hamilton in *Terminator 2*.

"Sorry I couldn't join you sooner," Betty said to the Hulk, "but I was making it clear to Major Jones's boss that, with the Super-Skrull running around, I wasn't going to idly stand by when I could be helping my husband." She patted the bulky pistol. "Besides, a girl can never be too careful in the big city." Before she married Bruce Banner, Betty was an "army brat." Her father was the late Thaddeus "Thunderbolt" Ross, a three-star general who had been a thorn in the Hulk's side for years. Often, it had been Betty's love for Banner that had prevented Ross from eliminating the Hulk once and for all.

Betty turned to Major Jones. "Colonel Morgan's still on board the SAFE helicarrier, but he's looking for an update on your Skrull hunt."

"Oh, I'm sure he's going to *love* to hear what I've got so far," said Jones, sarcastically. She nodded to Spidey, Whitmore, and the Hulk. "If you gentlemen will excuse me . . ." Turning on her heel, she strode toward the transport.

Betty stepped forward to shake Spider-Man's hand. "What are you doing here, Spider-Man—Bruce rope you into helping out?"

Spider-Man caught sight of the snide grin spreading across the Hulk's face. "Something like that, Mrs. Banner," he said. He gestured toward her fiery tresses. "You've, ah, changed since the last time I saw you."

Betty blew a puff of air to move a lock of hair that had fallen over her eyes. "When you're the wife of the

Hulk," she said, "you learn to change your appearance as often as possible. It keeps the hounds off the trail, so to speak." She sidled up to Spider-Man, her voice dropping to a conspiratorial whisper. "In case you didn't know, Bruce doesn't get along too well with the U.S. military."

"You don't say," said Spidey, acting shocked.

"I *do* say," replied Betty, grinning broadly. "But under the circumstances, SAFE has gotten clearance from the President to allow Bruce to help with the Super-Skrull's capture."

Spidey nodded. "So, now I know your beauty secrets." He gestured toward the Hulk. "But how do you keep *his* identity hidden—wrap him up in bandages?"

"Something like that," Betty said. She smiled. "At this point, putting some sort of super hero costume on him would just be a waste of time."

"I don't know . . ." Spidey said, thinking it over. "A big red cape, maybe an 'H' on his chest . . . he could be quite the fashion plate."

"Either that," said Betty, "or he'd be mistaken for the world's biggest Christmas decoration." She and Spidey laughed.

"What's so funny?" asked the Hulk, joining the duo.

Betty wiped away a tear of laughter. "We were just exchanging fashion tips," she said, smiling innocently.

"That shouldn't have taken too long," Whitmore remarked drily. "There are just so many things you can do with firearms and red-and-blue material."

As Whitmore continued his sarcastic commentary, Spider-Man's attention drifted back to the SAFE agents as they moved through the crowds, scanners probing the area for any sign of the Super-Skrull. He scratched the base of his skull.

I don't get it, he thought. *No real sign of trouble, but my spider-sense is still buzzing. If it's the Skrull, why doesn't he make his move? And if it's not, then where could he have gone?* Under his mask, Spider-Man frowned. *I've got a real bad feeling about this . . .*

A grizzled, bearded man in his forties walked out of a dark alleyway, heading west on Twenty-ninth Street. In one hand he carried a large metal suitcase. Battered trash cans and torn garbage bags—their contents spilled out on the pavement—lined the sidewalks, and scraps of yellowed paper blew across the potholed street. The stench of brine and dead fish wafted over from the Hudson River, fouling the hot summer air.

The man walked past boarded-up shops that stood in the shadow of the old West Side Highway, its overpass abandoned long ago and left to rust. A stray cat stepped out from between the rotted planks covering a store entrance, and spotted the man coming its way. The cat hissed an angry warning, its back arched high enough to give the animal the appearance of a dingy, black-and-gray horseshoe. Then the creature turned tail and ran back inside. The man paid no attention to it.

At the corner of Twenty-eighth Street was a battered, forlorn building. The red color of its brickface was long ago faded by decades of severe New York weather. Its entrance was a shabby, fly-specked door, above which hung a flickering neon sign that read

LAN DALE HOTEL

At some point in the building's history there had been an "S" in the sign, but the letter had fallen off and never been replaced.

The bearded man tromped up the dark, foul-smelling stairway to the second floor. The elderly woman at the front desk, completely absorbed by the events playing out on the evening soap opera she was watching, didn't bother to look up as he passed.

At the end of the half-lit hallway, the man entered Room 9 and bolted the door behind him. He placed the suitcase on the floor. Standing silently in the center of the room for a moment, he took a deep breath and closed his eyes. Suddenly, his form began to waver. The grizzled, middle-aged man faded from existence, replaced by a tall, six-hundred-pound warrior from another world.

Muscle hard as body armor shuddered under a skintight suit of purple and black. Green, hairless flesh stretched over heavy brows and a deeply furrowed chin. Bat-like ears—the most prominent feature of his cold, hate-filled face—flared in a great, sweeping arc, framing the alien skull.

K'lrt, the Super-Skrull, had returned to his true form.

K'lrt stood perfectly still, analyzing every sound, every movement outside his room. A baby cried hungrily two doors down. A man and woman argued loudly at the end of the hallway. The sounds of a television drama filtered through the thin walls between his room and the next. Nothing to concern him.

The Super-Skrull looked around the shabby room in which he'd been living for the past two days. Its wooden floors were worn and termite-weakened. Faded white curtains—tinged yellow by dirt and sunlight—hung in front of windows caked with grime. The bed—its mattress lumpy with age and barely large enough to accommodate a normal-sized person— sagged in the middle; obviously, the box spring was on its last legs. A single wooden straight-backed chair and a small chest of drawers were the only other furnishings. K'lrt's eyes blazed with white-hot fury. To think that a mighty Skrull warrior should be forced to live like this, like a . . . a human!

An eerie light shone from within the chest of drawers, filling the room with pale blue illumination. Quickly, the Super-Skrull crossed the room and opened the top drawer of the bureau. Reaching inside, he removed a device the size of a small flashlight. Blazing from its center was a blue-white crystal—the source of the light. Placing it on the floor, K'lrt stepped back, then dropped to one knee, his head bowed reverently.

The crystal pulsed rapidly, its energies swirling around the room. The Super-Skrull kept his head bowed, resisting the urge to look up. Slowly, a shape began forming in the blue-white whirlpool, quickly solidifying into a three-dimensional picture.

The image was of a woman dressed in opulent robes of black and dark blue hues, seated on a golden throne. A black skullcap rested comfortably on her hairless head. From her deeply furrowed chin and sweeping, bat-like ears, it was evident that she was a Skrull. But it was also clear that she was no ordinary Skrull female.

"What is your command, my Empress?" the Super-Skrull asked softly.

The Skrull Empress coolly observed K'lrt, her red eyes flashing with anger for just a moment. "Rise, K'lrt," she said. "Face me." K'lrt stood up. "Tell me,

"What is your command, my Empress?" the Super-Skrull asked softly.

my brave warrior," the Empress continued, "how goes your latest mission for the Empire?"

"I have run into some difficulty, my Empress," said K'lrt without hesitation.

The Empress smiled, but it was a smile as cold as death itself. "I see. And would this . . . 'difficulty,' as you describe it, have a name?"

K'lrt's eyebrow rose in a quizzical fashion. "I do not understand."

The Empress's lips pulled back in a snarl, revealing teeth that gleamed like daggers. "Come now, K'lrt," she said curtly. "Do you take your Empress for a fool?"

"Not at all, Empress!" replied the Super-Skrull.

"Yet you dare to stand before me and attempt to lie to my face!" The Empress laughed, a short note that sounded like ice breaking under a hammer's blow. "You are a bold one, K'lrt! Were that old fool, Dorrek, still on the throne, you would have easily convinced him of your sincerity!" The Empress thumped her chest with a gauntleted fist. "But I am not so easily gulled! Do you think that, after all your past transgressions, I would send you to Earth and not have you under observation the entire time?"

K'lrt's eyes widened in shock. " 'Under observation'—?"

"My spies are everywhere, K'lrt! I know of your failure, know of your clash with the human called Hulk, know of the timely interference by Spider-Man that averted your capture!" The Empress growled. "Pathetic. Pathetic and inexcusable. A Skrull infant could not have fared worse."

"Had the Hulk not been there to intercede, I would have succeeded in my task."

The Empress suppressed a yawn with a delicate hand. "You bore me, K'lrt. I have heard this useless chatter from you too often. At least *this* time you were wise enough to obey orders and break off your combat with the Hulk."

"It was behavior unfitting of a warrior," remarked the Super-Skrull. "It was . . . distasteful. Running from a battle only brings dishonor to me . . . and to the Empire."

"And to your Empress?" the sovereign asked, her voice sweet as poisoned honey. "We have had similar discussions before, K'lrt. As then, my word is final."

The Super-Skrull clenched his fists, leather gauntlets creaking in protest at the pressure. "Had you not ordered me to avoid conflict with all superpowered beings, I would have eliminated the Hulk and placed his cooling corpse at the foot of your throne."

"But that was not the point of your mission, was it, K'lrt?" the Empress shot back. She didn't wait for an answer. "No, of course it was not. Your mission was to remove a threat to the Skrull Empire. The Hulk is *not* that threat. But the one called Berkley Whitmore most certainly *is*." The sovereign leaned back in her throne.

"Correct me if my memory deserts me, K'lrt, but I recall that you have, at various times, promised to deliver the 'cooling corpses', as you put it, of the Silver Surfer, the Kree captain Mar-Vell, and the accursed Fantastic Four, among the many enemies of the Empire." The Empress frowned at K'lrt. "I am still waiting."

33

K'lrt gritted his teeth, fighting down the waves of anger that rippled through him. It would be futile to get into a heated argument with the Empress. Futile . . . and dangerous. Though her spies were acting merely as observers for now, they could quickly be turned into assassins at a command from their ruler, their only mission to execute K'lrt. Assassins who would strike without warning, from the shadows, from behind, never giving him an opportunity to die like a warrior.

And where would the honor be in that kind of death?

K'lrt relaxed, allowing the anger to slowly drain from his body. He lowered his head to break eye contact with the Empress, hoping that he looked suitably humbled.

"I . . . apologize for my outburst, Empress," he said, his voice a soft rumble. "I did not mean to question your orders."

The Empress nodded, satisfied with her subject's change in attitude. "Much better, K'lrt," she said. "It would be a pity to put you to death before you have an opportunity to redeem yourself to the Empire." Her gaze suddenly hardened, blood-red eyes blazing with the intensity of a raging fire. "But remember this, K'lrt: Defy my orders again, approach even the lowliest of these superpowered humans, and it shall give me the greatest pleasure to sign your death warrant. You are not on Earth to feed your ego. You are there to carry out a simple assassination." She sneered at K'lrt. "Even *you* should be able to handle that."

The Super-Skrull looked up to find the Empress pointing an accusatory finger at him. "Find Berkley Whitmore!" she ordered. "Kill him or, I swear by Sl'gur't, the god of war, you shall take Whitmore's place in death! Your name will become synonymous with failure and dishonor! And your soul will be trapped in limbo, never to join your fallen comrades in Val'kla'mor!"

"The Eternal Battle," the Super-Skrull whispered reverently. His dark green skin paled as the force of the Empress's words struck him.

From infancy, Skrulls were taught the ways of combat—to fight for the glory of the Skrull Empire, to die in the service of the Emperor or Empress. According to Skrull beliefs, when a warrior is killed in battle, his soul travels to Val'kla'mor, a realm where the afterlife is one continuous conflict. A fine reward for any Skrull who had died a proud, warrior's death. For a Skrull's soul to be denied entrance to Val'kla'mor is to be denied Paradise.

K'lrt drew himself up to his full height, back ramrod straight, head held high. "I will not fail you again, my Empress."

"There is no other option, K'lrt," said the Empress. "Succeed and have your honor restored. Fail and you become the shame of the Empire."

The Empress touched a control on her golden throne, breaking contact with the Super-Skrull. Her image wavered, then swirled into a whirlpool of blue-white energy. The light filling K'lrt's room dimmed as the crystal receiver cycled down, then fell silent.

Slowly, K'lrt's head drooped, his shoulders slumped, and his furrowed chin came to rest on his chest.

"Yes, my Empress," he whispered hoarsely to the darkness.

In a grimy and odorous room, on a planet far from home, the proud Skrull warrior felt very much alone.

CHAPTER
4

"**S**ure you've got enough there to eat, big guy?" asked Berkley Whitmore, eyeing a banquet-sized portion of food that the Hulk was consuming. Empty platters—enough to have served a dozen people—that once contained meats, fish, various pasta dishes and an assorted number of vegetables lay scattered across the single table occupied by the green giant. Whitmore, Spidey, and Betty Banner sat at an adjoining table, watching the devastation with awe.

The Hulk placed a massive hand over his mouth to suppress a belch. "Can I help it if I worked up an appetite chasing the Super-Skrull around the city?" he mumbled over a mouthful of steak and home fries. "Besides, if he shows up again, I won't have any trouble working it off."

Whitmore, the Hulk, Spider-Man, and Betty sat in the Platinum Towers Hotel's restaurant. Since a check of the building by fire marshals and city inspectors revealed no structural damage to the hotel or its wiring

"Sure you've got enough there to eat, big guy?" asked
Berkley Whitmore.

systems, the guests had been allowed to return to their rooms. The Hulk, opting for a "light snack," as he put it, had led the trio into the restaurant while the SAFE agents continued their sensor sweep of the area.

Spider-Man glanced around the restaurant as though looking for someone. Other than their small party, the only people in the restaurant were a waitress, a busboy, and a trio of SAFE agents stationed by the door.

This is starting to make me nuts, Spidey thought. *We're off the street and inside the hotel, and my spider-sense is still tingling. What is going on here?*

"Penny for your thoughts, Spider-Man?" asked Betty, having noticed his actions.

Spidey shook his head to clear the cobwebs. "It's kind'a hard to explain, Mrs. Banner—"

"Betty."

"All right . . . Betty," said Spidey. "There's something . . . not quite right here. I can't put my finger on it, but it's been nagging at me ever since we got to the hotel."

Whitmore leaned forward in his seat, looking seriously at Spidey. "Like what?"

Spidey shook his head. "I wish I could tell you, but I haven't a clue." He made a sweeping gesture across the room. "Everything seems all right . . . but it's not. There's something . . ." His voice trailed off, then he shrugged. "I don't know. Maybe I'm just seeing Skrulls where they're not."

"Understandable, given the situation," Betty said, sympathetically.

"I guess," said Spidey. He turned to the Hulk, who was washing down an entire apple pie with a gallon of milk. "Uh, hate to interrupt your snack, Doc, but could you clue me in on what happened before I came along?"

The Hulk daintily dabbed at the corners of his mouth with a napkin and pushed the table away from him, signalling the end of his meal. "Sure," he replied, settling back in his seat. The chair groaned under his immense weight.

"Well," the Hulk began, "it started a few days ago. Betty and I have been avoiding the authorities since my last . . . misunderstanding with them."

Spidey nodded. "I understand you're not too popular with the armed forces." He glanced at Betty, who giggled softly and raised a hand to cover her mouth.

"That's putting it mildly," said the Hulk. "Anyway, we were staying at a motel outside Orlando, Florida, when I heard the news about the awards ceremony for Berk."

"The kind of public back-patting I generally avoid," said Whitmore. "But given the cause, I was willing to make an exception."

The Hulk nodded in agreement. "And I wanted to be there to see Berk finally get the recognition he's deserved for his years of fighting for human rights."

"Of course," interjected Betty, "we couldn't just come breezing into New York and walk down the middle of Fifth Avenue in broad daylight. The last thing we needed was people getting the wrong impression that the incredible Hulk was on one of his legendary rampages." She paused for a moment, looked out the restaurant windows at the scores of law enforcement agents clogging the street. She turned back to the Hulk. "Guess that didn't last very long, huh, honey?"

The Hulk frowned at his wife. "Funny. Very funny."

"So how did you get into the city?" asked Spidey.

"We rented a van and I drove it up," said Betty. "Bruce stretched out in the back. Along the way, he called Berkley to let him know we were coming, and I dyed my hair red—I try not to keep one look for too long. When we arrived in Manhattan, it was late at night, so there weren't too many people in the hotel lobby. Berk had already arranged for a room for us under the names Mr. and Mrs. Ricardo."

"I have a fondness for *I Love Lucy*," added Whitmore.

"Didn't the front desk clerk get suspicious about an injured guest checking in?" asked Spidey.

The Hulk canted his head to one side, a look of confusion creeping across his features. " 'Injured guest'? Where'd you get that idea?"

"Well," said the web-spinner, "you couldn't have strolled in looking like you normally do, so I figure you must've been wearing bandages to hide your identity."

The Hulk shot a glance at Betty, who was smiling broadly. The jade giant grunted. "Anyway, Betty and I pretty much kept to our room until it was time for the awards dinner. It gave Berk and me a chance to catch up on old times."

"That's another thing I'm curious about," said Spider-Man. "How does a world-famous author like Berkley Whitmore get to be friends with the Hulk?"

"You talk to him in one-syllable words," said Whitmore. He flashed a wry grin at the Hulk, then looked back to Spidey. "A few years back, I was living in an apartment down on the lower East Side. Not the choicest spot in the city to hang your hat, but the landlady was a real sweetheart and she worked hard to keep the building running."

"April Sommers," the Hulk said wistfully, staring off into space. Betty shot him a razor-edged glance that snapped him out of his daydream. "She was an actress and model, but it was strictly a landlord/tenant situation, honey." He crossed his heart with a thick green finger. "Honest."

"So, you guys were roommates?" asked Spidey. "That must have been interesting. Talk about your odd couples."

"Not roomies," said Whitmore, shaking his mane of reddish hair. "Neighbors. Bruce rented a room down the hall from me and, after running into each other a few times, we started talking. He was the first person I'd run into there who had more than a spoonful of intelligence."

"Thanks, Berk," said the Hulk. "I think."

"Of course," continued Whitmore, "I didn't know who he really was. This was back in the days when he looked like an average, skinny, nerdy guy . . . except he'd get all big and green when you made him angry."

The Hulk nodded. "No one liked me when I was angry." Turning to Spidey, he pointed a thumb at Whitmore. "A short fuse is one of the things we have in common. The only difference is that Berk doesn't turn green."

"As far as you know," quipped Whitmore. He brushed a piece of lint from his jacket sleeve.

Silently, Spidey studied Whitmore. The advantage of wearing a mask that covered his entire head meant that Spidey could appear to be looking right at the Hulk when he was actually observing the author.

I don't get it, the wall-crawler thought. *My spider-sense has been droning along ever since I met Whitmore. Could he be the one setting it off?* He watched the author conversing with the Hulk and Betty, noticed how at ease Whitmore was around the jade giant. Spidey frowned. *No, it couldn't be him. What kind of threat could he be to me? He's got a reputation for taking a poke at people who get on his bad side, but it's never been without just cause. And I seriously doubt that a guy who makes a scarecrow look overweight would be a problem for me.*

Spidey's gaze shifted over to the green behemoth. *Maybe it's the Hulk. Doc Banner's never been at the top of my list of people I trust, especially given our past confrontations. My spider-sense could be reacting to his proximity—not too strong because he doesn't pose an immediate threat, not too weak because he's right in front of me.* He looked out the window to see Major Jones's men making their rounds. It didn't appear they were having much success in their search for Skrulls. *Or maybe the Super-Skrull is just biding his time, waiting for the right moment to attack . . .*

Whitmore turned to Spidey. "It didn't take us long to become friends. Bruce was trying to put some order into his otherwise chaotic life by renting an apartment, finding a job, learning to relax so his more . . . savage nature wouldn't hold sway."

The Hulk chuckled. "The fact that I didn't lose my temper during some of our more heated arguments—"

"Debates," interjected Whitmore.

"—is something akin to a miracle," finished the Hulk.

"I, on the other hand," said Whitmore, "was up to

my eyeballs with the manuscript for *The Reality of Evil*. A monster of a book that I wasn't able to finish for another two years."

"The one about the Judans and Myndai," said Spidey. "It blew me away. I can't remember the last time I've read something that powerful."

"A thinly-veiled allegory for World War II and the treatment of political prisoners." Whitmore sneered. "The publisher insisted I had to write it as a science-fiction novel so readers wouldn't be too disturbed by the content. People don't like being reminded of how cruel they can often be." He snorted in disgust.

"Can I ask you something that I've always been wondering about?" inquired Spidey. "You've probably been hit with this question a million times."

"Go right ahead, my web-headed friend," Whitmore said with an encouraging wave of his hand.

"How were you able to write it from the perspective of the commander of the Myndai prisoner of war camp? It felt like you were right inside the guy's head."

Whitmore said nothing. He closed his eyes, as though trying to block out something he didn't want to see, then opened them again. Staring at the table before him, he moved his index finger in a circular motion on the white cloth covering. He cleared his throat, but did not look up at Spider-Man.

"It's been said that everyone has a dark side, a place inside us all where our blackest, most disturbing thoughts live, waiting for release." Whitmore nodded toward the Hulk. "That was made clear to Bruce the night that gamma bomb exploded and loosed *his* dark half—the Hulk—on the world. In the case of the book, I had to tap into a part of me I'd been repressing for years. A part that needed liberation before the pressure killed me." His expression softened, and a melancholy smile turned up the corners of his mouth. "I guess my side's a bit darker than others'."

"My late uncle used to say that 'with great power comes great responsibility'," said Spidey. "But your book made it so clear that it's not just responsibility that makes a man honorable, but his *deeds*. A few years ago, when I was feeling sorry for myself and thinking about giving up the whole web-swinging bit, your words made me realize that everything I'd done with my powers—the people I've helped, the lives I've touched—was worth the struggle. It changed how I thought about myself." He paused. "I've always wanted to thank you for that."

Whitmore looked at Spider-Man, for once at a loss for words. "You're . . . welcome," he finally said, a smile slowly coming to his lips. "It's nice to hear my work considered more than just words on a page."

The Hulk softly cleared his throat. "That reminds me, Berk. How come *I* never got a copy of that book?"

"Well, if you'd stayed in one place long enough for me to get an address, I would've sent you one," said Whitmore. "Before today, the last time I saw you was when you were whisked off the front stoop by government thugs." He turned to Spidey. "There I am, struggling through chapter ten of *Evil*, when all of a sudden there's this light outside my window as bright as a nuclear explosion. Well, when you've got an interruption of that magnitude going on, of course you're not gonna get any work done—you have to go see what's the matter. I look outside and what do I see? Bruce getting yanked into the sky by some kind of energy beam!"

"It was a vortex beam," the Hulk explained. "Thunderbolt Ross and his amazing army of Hulkbusters, up to their old tricks." He glanced at Betty. "No offense, honey."

"None taken," said Betty. "I'm well aware of how . . . single-minded Dad was in those days."

The Hulk nodded. "Anyway, they tracked me down to the apartment building and kidnapped me right in front of April."

"And that was the last I saw of Bruce until last night," said Whitmore.

"And the Super-Skrull?" asked Spidey.

"Well, I'm stumped about the whole matter," replied Whitmore. "I'd never seen *him* before in my entire life. I was just about to give my acceptance speech at the dinner—and let me tell you, if you're ever invited to an awards dinner, don't go 'cause the food is always, *always* lousy—when one of the waiters pulls out the mother of all handguns and takes a shot at me! Me! Can you believe it? A guy who wouldn't harm a fly . . . unless it kept buzzing around my head, that is." He shook his head. "You'd think I made a bad comment about the service."

"That's when I jumped in," the Hulk added. "Betty and I were sitting off to the side, so as not to bring attention to ourselves. From the corner of my eye, I caught a glint of something metallic in the waiter's hand, and it wasn't a serving tray. Just as he pulled out his gun, I leaped across the room and landed in front of Berk to shield him. The weapon's discharge was phenomenal—it was like being slammed by the

Thing." He rubbed the dark edges of a hole burned in the center of his frayed dress shirt. "If the blaster power had hit Berk instead of me . . ."

"Seeing Bruce get shot was a shock," Betty commented. "I tried charging the gunman, but the audience was in a panic, running every whichway. I couldn't get near him. And then he started to . . . change." She shuddered involuntarily, clearly disturbed by the memory. "That's when we found out he was the Super-Skrull."

Whitmore snorted. "He screamed, 'Death to the enemies of the Skrull Empire!' and fired off a few more rounds, not giving Bruce any time to fight back. Then the Skrull called Bruce a few nasty names and, seeing that he wasn't about to succeed in killing me, ran out through the service entrance."

"You know the rest," said the Hulk.

Spidey mulled over the information. "And you have no idea," he said to Whitmore, "why the Super-Skrull would want you dead?"

"None whatsoever," Whitmore insisted. He shrugged. "Maybe he doesn't like my writing. Maybe it's my hair, or the way I dress. When you've angered as many people as I have over the years, you stop trying to figure out what makes them wackos." He smiled. "But then, you'd know all about that, wouldn't you, Spider-Man?"

"True," agreed Spidey. "But I doubt it's as simple as that. We're talking about a guy who's gone toe-to-toe with entire groups of super heroes, who's died and come back enough times to make my head spin. No offense, Mr. Whitmore—"

"Berkley," Whitmore said. "My *father* is Mr. Whitmore."

"—but you don't exactly appear to be a threat to the Skrull Empire."

During all this banter, Betty had remained silent, the look of concentration on her face so intense it seemed she was burning a hole in the floor with her stare. She leaned forward to join the conversation.

"Maybe," said Betty, "he wasn't out to destroy Berkley, but rather what Berk represents."

"Opinionated, arrogant writers everywhere?" asked the Hulk, needling his old friend.

Whitmore scowled at the green behemoth. "Don't you have a 'puny human' to smash somewhere?"

Betty shook her head. "No, no. I mean that Berkley is famous for his stance on human rights issues, correct?" All three men nodded in agreement. "He's been spreading the word for twenty-five years now about how we should stop the mistreatment of political prisoners around the world." Again, nods. "Well, what if his message has reached *beyond* the Earth? What if, right now, on some planet controlled by the Skrull Empire, there are people fighting for the same kind of cause, spurred on by his words?"

The Hulk rubbed his face with a calloused hand. "Now, Betty, Berk has enough of a swelled head already. Don't go giving him the idea that he's influencial on a *universal* level."

"It makes sense, though," said Spidey. "In a way. If the Skrull was sent here to assassinate Berkley, it would remove the threat he was talking about."

"It's a ridiculous notion!" exclaimed Whitmore. "If that lantern-jawed moron actually succeeded in killing me, it'd only make me a martyr to the cause. These hypothetical people Betty was talking about would only fight harder to bring about changes in the political system. The Empire would be in worse shape than when it started!"

"That's true, Berk," said the Hulk. "Then again, Skrulls have never been known to look at the big picture before launching into their campaigns."

Any further discussion was cut short as Betty pointed toward the windows. "What's going on out there?"

As Betty spoke, Spidey leaped up from his chair, his spider-sense flaring like a jolt of electricity scorching his body. "Trouble!" he said. "Big time!" He leaped over the table and landed by the windows.

On the street, police officers were hurriedly moving the crowd nearest the hotel even further back than before. Left behind in the wake of the stampeding humanity were a group of SAFE agents, led by Nefretiti Jones, who were chasing an overweight man in his forties. The man looked obviously distressed by the black-clad men and women who pounded down the street after him, their hands hovering above the butts of their guns. The agents, however, were not focused on the man's reactions . . . *but on the oversized suitcase he carried.*

"It's the Super-Skrull!" exclaimed Spider-Man. "He's come back!"

CHAPTER

5

Spidey bounced across the restaurant toward the nearest exit. Right behind him charged the Hulk, who turned to point at the SAFE agents guarding the entrance.

"Keep an eye on Whitmore!" he ordered. "This could be a ruse!"

Unholstering their weapons, the agents formed a protective ring around the author and Betty. A look of concern crossed her features as she watched her husband dash out the door, and she reflexively moved her right hand closer to the weapon in the shoulder holster under her left arm.

Out on Forty-sixth Street, Spidey and the Hulk burst through a fire exit to find the SAFE agents turning the corner as they chased the overweight man onto Sixth Avenue.

"For a guy that size, he's sure light on his feet," Spidey remarked to the Hulk. Jumping into the air,

Spidey fired a web-line to a nearby lamppost and swung after the agents. "Come on, Doc!" he yelled back. "The game's afoot!"

"Right behind you!" said the Hulk. He ran to catch up, his footfalls sending small tremors rippling through the pavement.

Ahead of the two heroes, the SAFE agents were closing in on their quarry. Glancing over his shoulder, the man saw his pursuers no more than a dozen yards behind him. Muttering angry comments in an incomprehensible language, he reached under his dark gray blazer and pulled out a formidable-looking weapon—the kind of gun usually seen in science-fiction films. Within the wide barrel glowed a harsh red light.

"Gun!" cried Jones.

The man fired, the roar of the weapon booming like cannon fire. SAFE agents and pedestrians dove for cover as an energy blast tore a wide hole in the sidewalk. Shattered fragments of concrete rained down like confetti.

Spider-Man and the Hulk were just reaching the corner of Forty-seventh Street when the blast struck. Firing both web-shooters, Spidey created a safety net above Sixth Avenue that caught most of the falling debris.

"Somebody's getting a ticket for littering," the web-slinger commented drily.

"Get back!" yelled Jones, waving frantically at the shocked civilians around her. She didn't need to repeat that order. Businessmen and theatergoers, teenagers and adults, rich and poor alike scattered like frightened rabbits seeking the security of their hutches.

The man fired his gun a second time. The blast narrowly missed Jones's head, striking instead a car parked at the curb twenty feet behind her. The car's gas tank, overheated by the intensity of the energy beam, exploded. The concussive force of the detonation threw a pair of SAFE agents into the air and across Sixth Avenue. Jones watched, horrified, as her men soared above the snarled evening traffic, their trajectory taking them on a path that would slam them against a building on the opposite side of the street. Though members of SAFE wore lightweight body armor underneath their dark uniforms, it was unlikely the two agents would survive the impact.

Just as the duo were about to strike the wall, a figure clad in a familiar red-and-blue costume swung down and caught them. Using his own body as a shield, Spider-Man took the brunt of the collision with his back. Though winded and slightly dazed, he held onto the agents as he dropped to the sidewalk, landing delicately on the balls of his toes. Laying the agents on the pavement, Spider-Man checked to see that they were all right. He gave an encouraging wave to Jones.

"Elfman!" Jones called out. "See to our people!"

"On it, ma'am!" Elfman said. He hurried across the avenue to take charge of the injured duo.

Major Jones breathed a sigh of relief, allowing herself a brief smile. Then her expression turned cold and, eyes flashing with anger, she looked for the man they'd been chasing. Their quarry, gun still in hand, had reached the corner of Forty-ninth Street, where he recklessly dashed into the northbound flow of traffic, narrowly avoiding being struck by a pizza delivery van. Brakes squealed and metal crunched as cars and trucks came to an abrupt halt. Horns blared, and drivers yelled at the man as he dodged through the jam. Sixth Avenue was turning into a carbon copy of the earlier situation on Broadway.

"Fine. We'll do it the hard way," said Jones, grimly. She motioned to her agents, who unholstered their guns. "Heat 'em up!" she barked. The air filled with the high-pitched whine of miniature laser-generators cycling up to speed. Leaping to her feet, Jones led her troops after the fleeing man. Bystanders ran for cover as it became evident that a shoot-out was about to take place in the middle of Manhattan.

Rejoining the chase, Spider-Man swung over the snarl of traffic and shook his head. "Traffic jams. Skrulls with suitcases. People waving guns. Isn't this where I came in?"

Ricochetting from car to truck to bus, he again caught up to the chase. A half-block behind him stomped the Hulk, who was attempting to be less destructive than he had been on Broadway. Carefully easing between cars slowed down the green behemoth, but at least he wasn't endangering—or angering—any more drivers.

Something's wrong here, thought Spidey, watching the overweight man push his way through teeming crowds of bystanders. *If that's the Super-Skrull, why isn't he using his powers? Why does he seem so afraid? He may've run from a fight with the Hulk earlier, but it wouldn't make him act like—*

His spider-sense suddenly jangled like a school bell, and Spider-Man looked down to see the man turning around . . . and aiming his gun directly at the wall-crawler!

"EEYOWWW!!" cried Spidey as a crimson burst of

"EEYOWWW!!" cried Spidey as a crimson burst of superheated energy sliced through his webbing, inches from his head.

superheated energy sliced through his web-line, inches from his head.

Wordlessly, the man fired again and again at the web-slinger. But, between Spidey's warning sense and the hero's acrobatic abilities, there was no chance of the man actually hitting him.

With blinding speed, Spider-Man executed a series of moves that would make an Olympic-level gymnast envious, each twist and turn bringing him closer to his target. The man cursed and fired wildly, the shots striking street signs, lampposts, traffic signals—everything but the colorfully-garbed super hero.

Bouncing off the top of a billboard that was being driven through the streets by a green minivan, Spider-Man gracefully flipped above the man and fired both web-shooters. With a resounding *thwap!,* thick strands of webbing adhered to the barrel of the gun. Spidey landed on the side of a building and pulled sharply on the web-lines. The gun flew from the man's hands and into Spidey's.

"Hey, is this one of those rare, collectible Flash Gordon ray guns like they used to use in those old movie serials?" asked Spidey. He crumpled the weapon into a rough ball-shape as though it was made of tin foil. "Oops. Hope it wasn't real valuable."

"Bah!" growled the man. He turned and ran.

Jones pointed at the man as she turned to her agents. "Take him down!" she commanded. "Full stun!" Assuming firing stances, the SAFE members brought their guns to bear on the man.

Great, thought Spidey. *You take away one kid's gun, and suddenly everybody else has to use theirs. You'd think having Whitmore read the riot act to them before would've made an impression . . .*

"Major! Hold your fire!" Spidey yelled to Jones as he jumped from the building he'd been clinging to and landed on the roof of a bus. "I think you've got the wrong man . . . or at least the wrong Skrull!"

"What are you talking about?" said Jones.

"Give me a minute and you'll see!" Firing a web-line, Spidey leaped off the bus and swung after the man, who was running toward the neon lights and glittering marquee of Radio City Music Hall. Unfortunately for the man, a jazz concert had ended minutes before, and the sidewalk was packed with exiting patrons. Hampered by the slow-moving crowd that flowed around him like molasses, as well as by the weight of his suitcase, the man's flight came to a quick end.

Landing on the music hall marquee, Spidey shot out a pair of web-lines that adhered to the man's shoulders. With a powerful tug, the wall-crawler yanked him into the air and onto the marquee. The man landed on his back with a dull *thud*, the impact forcing him to release the suitcase. Moving swiftly, Spidey wrapped him from shoulders to feet in thick layers of webbing.

"Hey! I caught a big one!" Spidey said.

The man snarled at him. "Cretin! Primitive! Human scum!"

"I bet you say that to all the card-carrying super heroes," said Spidey. He picked up the man, cradling him under one arm, then retrieved the suitcase. "If you don't mind, I have some friends I'd like you to meet. I'm sure they'd like to ask you a few questions."

"They will learn nothing from me!" the man bellowed. "Filthy—"

"Yeah, yeah, 'human scum,' " snapped Spidey. "Get a new insult, would you?"

Stepping to the edge of the marquee, Spidey jumped down, bounced off the cab of a truck, and landed on the sidewalk. The Hulk, Major Jones, and the SAFE agents ran up to join the web-slinger and his burden.

"Nice going, Spider-Man," complimented Jones. "We'll take it from here." She motioned to her team. A pair of SAFE agents took hold of the prisoner, who struggled against the synthetic webbing that encased him. "We'd better not take any chances with this one," said the major. Jones turned to a willowy Hispanic woman with blond hair. "Montenegro—the sedative-ray."

Reaching to her belt, Montenegro unclipped a small device shaped like a tape dispenser and pressed a button on its side. The tip of the device glowed a soft purple.

The man fought even harder to free himself. "Fools! Miscreants!" he screamed. "You are all doomed!"

Jones stepped forward, her nose just inches from the prisoner's face. "If you don't behave, I'll have Spider-Man web up your mouth . . . and then I'll turn you over to Doctor Banner."

The green-skinned scientist smiled wickedly and cracked his knuckles. The sound was like the report of a high-powered rifle.

The man stopped fighting instantly. Montenegro moved up and pressed the barrel of the contrivance against his neck. A beam of light lanced out, and the man slumped in the arms of the agents.

"Di-i-i-i-e . . . you'll all . . . die . . ." he droned groggily.

"Pretty effective do-hickey," commented Spidey to Jones. "Where'd you get it?"

"Another Reed Richards invention," said Jones. "Developed for the Avengers when they were involved in the Kree-Skrull War. It keeps Skrulls too woozy to cause any trouble."

"Think I could borrow one of those for a few days?" asked Spidey. "I know a few bad guys *I'd* like to keep woozy for a while."

Jones smiled briefly and wagged a finger at the web-slinger. "These aren't toys, Spider-Man."

"You sure about that? I could swear I found one just like it in a box of cere—"

"Look," the Hulk said huffily, stepping between Spidey and the Major, "I'm sure you two find this banter fascinating, but some of us have wives to get back to." He gestured with a thumb toward the prisoner. "You know, if you'd excuse us for a few minutes, Major, I'm sure I can . . . persuade your prisoner to answer *any* questions. I'm *much* more effective than a tranquilizer."

"I can't allow that, Doctor Banner," said Jones, shaking her head. "If we're going to find out what this is all about, I need this man in one piece."

"So, tell me the piece you want, and I'll leave it alone," growled the Hulk. "But *I* get the rest."

The man's eyes widened in horror. "Y-you would not dare . . . !" He looked to Jones. "Please! Keep him away from me!"

Jones chuckled. "Reed Richards was right. Push a

Skrull hard enough and he starts to cave in under the pressure."

The Hulk rubbed his jaw, obviously confused by the man's reaction. He leaned forward to study the prisoner, staring hard into the man's eyes.

"You're not the Super-Skrull, are you?" he asked.

"That's what *I* figure, Doc," said Spidey.

"How's that, Spider-Man?" asked Jones.

"Well, he doesn't *act* like the Super-Skrull, for one thing," replied Spidey. "Even though he ran away the last time, I doubt the Super-Skrull would bolt a second time—his ego wouldn't allow it. And he didn't even try to use any of his Fantastic Four abilities—his Human Torch powers would've burned away my webs in a second. Besides, if it really came down to a battle between SAFE and the Super-Skrull, I don't think your men would be the ones who'd come out on top." He looked at the gathered agents. "No offense, guys."

"Then who *is* he?" asked Jones.

"Let's find out," said the Hulk, eagerly. Grasping the man by the lapels of his jacket, the jade giant hoisted him up to eye-level, pulled the man close to his face, and growled. "Show-and-tell time, friend."

The man's features blurred like a picture out of focus. Flesh contorted, flowed like water, and began reshaping. Pale-white skin tone turned a dark green hue. Bones crackled, shifted, re-knitted into a familiar shape. Bat-like ears sprouted and a knobby chin took form. In seconds, the man had changed into a Skrull warrior!

The Hulk was unimpressed by the transformation. "You have a name, friend?" It wasn't a question, but a demand.

"I am . . . Durklan," the Skrull said sullenly. "I am known as 'He-Who-Strikes-From-the-Shadows.' "

"A pleasure to meet you, Durklan," said the Hulk. "I am Bruce Banner, usually referred to as the incredible Hulk: He-Who-Smashes-with-His-Fists." He gestured toward Nefertiti Jones. "She is Major Jones, She-Who-Could-Have-You-Shot-at-Dawn." The Hulk waved a hand at Spidey. "And this is Spider-Man, He-Who-Thinks-with-His-Mouth."

"Gee, thanks, Doc," said Spidey.

The Hulk glared at Durklan. "Now that the introductions are out of the way, would you mind telling us what you're doing here, and what's in the suitcase?"

The Skrull stared angrily at the Hulk, saying nothing. The Hulk raised a meaty fist in front of the prisoner's face.

"If you make me angry," he warned, "you'll be known far and wide as Durklan, He-Whose-Spine-is-Shaped-Like-a-Pretzel."

The Skrull looked from the Hulk's face to his massive fist and back to his face. Durklan sighed. "Very well. Unlike my brothers in the warrior caste, I am not interested in experiencing pain in any form, even for the glory of the Empire." The Hulk chuckled softly and lowered his hand. Durklan nodded toward the suitcase. "It contains surveillance equipment."

"You're a spy?" asked Spidey.

"An assassin!" crowed the Skrull, obviously pleased with his career choice. "Hand-picked by the Empress herself! Why, if you only knew of the great number of enemies I have slain to protect the Empire, you would treat me with far greater respect!"

"Shut up," ordered the Hulk. Durklan did as he was told.

"But, you're carrying around surveillance equipment, so you were sent to spy on somebody," said Spidey. "Who? Berkley Whitmore?"

The Skrull remained silent. The Hulk sighed. He reached out with a massive paw and calmly put it around the Skrull's throat. Then he applied the slightest pressure. The Skrull's eyes began to bulge in their sockets.

"Okay," said the Hulk. "Here's what we're going to do. I'll let you go in a moment, and I'll allow you one deep breath. But before you take a second, I want to hear the answer to Spider-Man's question, or I'm going to squeeze until your brain pops out through your skull." He winked slyly at Spider-Man. "Or is that Skrull?" The Hulk looked back to Durklan. "Do you understand?"

The Skrull nodded eagerly. His face was turning unnatural shades of deep green and purple under the pressure from the Hulk's hold.

The Hulk relaxed his grip, showing a friendly, toothy smile to the Skrull. "Go on," said the jade giant.

Durklan gasped, grateful for the opportunity to breathe once more. He shook his head. "Not Whitmore," said the Skrull. "I was merely keeping watch over him for the time being. My real assignment is K'lrt . . . the one you know as Super-Skrull."

Jones was stunned. "But, why? He's one of your own people."

"Bah!" spat Durklan. "He is no longer one of my people. He is a failure! Too often has he been humiliated by you humans. He has fallen out of favor with our Empress, questioned her commands once too often. My instructions were to see to it that he carries out the elimination of this Whitmore."

"And if he should fail to do that," said the Hulk, "then your orders are to kill the Super-Skrull, right? After all, you *are* an assassin—that's your job, to kill people." Durklan said nothing. The Hulk nodded. "Just as I thought."

"But why does the Empress want Whitmore dead?" asked Spider-Man.

Durklan shrugged. "I do not know." He glanced at the Hulk, who looked as though he didn't believe that. "I swear it is the truth. I am only given enough information to enable me to carry out my assignment."

Jones stroked her chin, looking deep in thought. "It makes sense," she said. "That way, if he's captured, he can't jeopardize the mission by leaking too many of the facts."

"So, he can't tell us why the Super-Skrull wants to kill Berk," concluded the Hulk, "but I bet he knows where we can find him." He grinned menacingly at Durklan. "Don't you?"

The Skrull swallowed nervously.

CHAPTER
6

In a filthy, darkened hotel room in the shadow of the West Side Highway, the Super-Skrull sat wearily on the edge of his bed. He could not rest, could not banish the fury that surged through every fiber of his being.

It seemed a hundred lifetimes ago since K'lrt had been one of the most honored officers in the Skrull Empire. Yet, only a few short years had passed since that glorious time. He had led invasion forces against countless worlds, defeated countless armies, all in the name of the Empire. From Andromeda to the Greater Magellanic Cloud to the edges of the Shi'ar Empire, innumerable races lived in fear of the day when great Skrull battleships would gather around their worlds, waiting to strike.

Waiting to destroy.

K'lrt had had the honor of commanding such fleets during his illustrious career. How proud, how noble, how self-confident he had been then! The universe was his for the taking, and he wanted it all!

Sitting in the darkness, K'lrt's thoughts drifted back to a time when his future seemed to blaze as brightly as a guiding star . . .

The Empire had been growing in leaps and bounds. The Kree—the alien race that had ruthlessly attacked the Empire millions of years ago and started the Skrulls down the path of aggression—continued to cause trouble, but posed no immediate threat. Skrull engineers had converted all ten worlds of the Kral system into an amusement and resort center for the entertainment of the Empire's most rich and powerful citizens. Emperor Dorrek was leading the Empire into a new Golden Age.

That's when the problems with Earth began.

For centuries, Skrull spies had been journeying to Earth, using their shapeshifting abilities to observe the planet's inhabitants. But they always dreaded the day when humans would develop the technology that would allow them to venture into space . . . and become a threat to the Empire. A threat that would have to be eliminated.

That concern was realized in the mid-twentieth century with the development of the American and Russian space programs. Skrull spies watched closely as the two superpowers raced to be the first to put a man into orbit around the planet, then to place a man on the moon. The spies reported these events to the Emperor, waiting for his command to sabotage mankind's efforts to reach the stars.

But Dorrek saw no reason to interfere, certain that

the Earth presented no threat to his Empire. While it was true that humans had developed limited space travel, they had never succeeded in going beyond their own lifeless satellite. The Skrulls, on the other hand, had developed long-range flight centuries ago, and had created mighty weapons far more powerful than anything ever devised on Earth. The Skrull Empire was safe . . . until the day came when superpowered humans began appearing across the planet.

It began with the Fantastic Four, a quartet of adventurers—Reed Richards, Ben Grimm, Susan Storm, and her younger brother, Johnny—who had been irradiated by a powerful dose of cosmic rays during the test flight of an experimental starship. Other heroes—some created by radiation like the FF, some born with extraordinary abilities—soon followed: Spider-Man. The incredible Hulk. The Avengers. The X-Men. The Age of the Super Hero had arrived.

The Skrull Emperor began to worry. Something had to be done.

Dispatching four of his best warriors to Earth, Dorrek ordered them to impersonate the Fantastic Four. Their aim was to commit crimes and destroy property while disguised as the heroes, giving the appearance that the foursome had turned into super-villains. The plan almost succeeded, until Richards realized that a group of shape-changers were behind the criminal acts. Capturing three of the Skrulls, Richards hypnotized and ordered them to assume new, peaceful identities. They became cows.

When word of this defeat reached the Emperor, Dorrek flew into a rage. Skrulls beaten by humans! It was unacceptable! In response, he ordered his top scientists

Sitting in the darkness, K'lrt's thoughts drifted back . . .

to create a superhumanoid Skrull warrior whose abilities could match those of the Fantastic Four. The project nearly drained the royal treasury.

At the time, K'lrt was an ambitious, heavily decorated soldier, one admired by the more powerful families in the Empire. His career was on the rise. When the day came for his retirement from the military, it was expected that he would enter the political arena, where his following would grow.

Dorrek was well aware of K'lrt's rising status, but he couldn't simply have the warrior eliminated. Such a move could cause dissension, and then the Emperor would be fighting off a constant line of usurpers attempting to seize the throne. No, a more subtle solution was needed—one that would play to K'lrt's oversized ego and afford the Emperor the opportunity to remove this potential threat. And then the Emperor hit upon a plan.

K'lrt would become Dorrek's instrument of revenge.

K'lrt's feats as a warrior were heralded throughout the Empire. His dedication to his Emperor was as passionate as his love of combat. He was a proud Skrull who would not bow to lesser beings, who would crush these humans like the insects they were in comparison to his superior race of shapeshifters. K'lrt was a Skrull who obeyed orders without question, who allowed duty and honor to blind him to events going on around him. The perfect warrior. The perfect follower.

The perfect dupe.

K'lrt was more than willing to undergo the operations that bionically augmented his strength, and the doses of cosmic radiation that allowed him to mimic the Fantastic Four's unique abilities. Power-receptors designed to absorb additional cosmic energy were implanted throughout his body. There were times when K'lrt was certain that the countless modifications to his body would kill him. There were even times when he felt as though death was preferable to the constant pain he suffered. But he endured.

After months of surgery and training, the scientists finally gathered before Dorrek to proudly unveil the fruits of their labors. The Emperor now had his superwarrior. His champion.

His Super-Skrull.

With the blessing of the Emperor—who was glad to see him leave—K'lrt departed for Earth to claim the planet in the name of the Empire. Should the Fantastic Four attempt to interfere, his orders were simple: kill them. But K'lrt's mission soon turned out to be more complicated than even Dorrek had anticipated.

Arriving on Earth, K'lrt soon found himself in heated battle with the FF. He was able to make quick work of the quartet, beating them soundly with their own powers.

However, in analyzing the manner in which K'lrt had attacked the family of super heroes, Reed Richards realized that the Super-Skrull's strength was being increased by cosmic energy rays transmitted to Earth through a warp in space. K'lrt's powers were being beamed to him from the heart of the Skrull Empire!

By goading the Super-Skrull into a rematch, the FF were able to lure K'lrt to a remote island in the Pacific Ocean. Once there, they imprisoned him in a mountain, sealing the entrance and blocking K'lrt from the energy beam. Cut off from all cosmic energy, K'lrt remained a prisoner until, months later, a more powerful energy beam was created by Skrull scientists. The improved beam was able to penetrate the tons of rock around K'lrt and restore his strength.

K'lrt tried to redeem himself to the Emperor by battling the Fantastic Four a second time, only to be defeated. This time, the indignity was doubled for K'lrt, as he became a bargaining chip in a prisoner exchange between the Fantastic Four and the Emperor. He was swapped in return for Sue and Johnny's father, Franklin Storm, who had been taken captive by other Skrulls.

In his darkened hotel room, K'lrt thought back to that day, his eyes burning with the memory of that humiliation.

How Dorrek had crowed when his once-proud warrior was brought home in chains! And yet, he was willing to give the Super-Skrull one more chance. After all, the honor of the Empire was at stake.

K'lrt returned to Earth, where he clashed with the brash thunder god named Thor. Again, the Super-Skrull met with defeat. He fled back to Tarnax IV, the Imperial Throneworld, in disgrace.

It was the end of K'lrt's distinguished military career. The medals and honors he had gathered for his years of service meant nothing. Any political aspirations he may have had were gone. His enemies hadn't even allowed him to die with dignity.

It was more than Dorrek could have hoped for.

Having the now-humbled warrior brought before him, Dorrek took great pleasure in informing K'lrt that, for his many failures, for the shame he had brought to the Empire, for his inability to subjugate mere humans, he was to be banished. Exiled. Banned from admittance to any world in the Empire.

K'lrt had thought about taking his own life, but there was no honor in suicide. He became a wanderer, aimlessly traveling from star system to star system, feared by some races, despised by most. His hatred kept him alive—hatred of the Emperor, and of the humans who had caused his downfall. Most of all, though, he hated himself. He was a failure, and admitted it . . . if only to his reflection in a mirror. He lived without purpose for years.

When Dorrek was eventually assassinated by his own wife, R'kill, K'lrt was called back to active duty, where he led a number of missions to Earth in various attempts to destroy the planet. But defeats at the hands of the Hulk, the Sub-Mariner, Spider-Man, Ms. Marvel, and the Silver Surfer again jeopardized his career. K'lrt felt the shadow of failure wrapping itself around him. Another sentence of exile would be more than he could bear.

But before K'lrt could be punished, the world-eater Galactus arrived in the Empire . . . and devoured the Imperial Throneworld. R'kill, her daughter, Princess Anelle, and millions of Skrulls were killed.

When he heard the news, K'lrt—who once would have laid down his life for the Empire—*laughed*.

After a period of civil war, a new Empress was crowned. Again, K'lrt was restored to his former military position, and again he was beaten by superpowered humans.

The last straw, though, was when he disobeyed a royal command. In a battle with the Silver Surfer, it appeared that K'lrt had been killed by the captain of an alien vessel. The Empress wanted K'lrt to go along with this subterfuge, for reasons she kept to herself.

The Super-Skrull objected. Allowing a lower lifeform to think that he had killed the Empire's greatest warrior was outrageous. K'lrt felt dishonored. But the Empress wasn't interested in his bruised ego. She ordered him to bear his shame in private.

But after years of failures and punishments, honor was all K'lrt had left. His mind was in turmoil: His oath of fealty dictated that he serve the Empress, no matter how distasteful her orders might be, but his personal code of honor demanded satisfaction for the disgrace he had been ordered to endure. He needed guidance.

Traveling to the temple of Sl'gur't, K'lrt begged the war god for a sign, something that would show him the path he should take to resolve this inner conflict. The sensation of the temple's cool air and cold jade floor against his skin had a soothing effect on the warrior. He relaxed, allowing his thoughts to drift. And then K'lrt's mind flooded with understanding.

Death before dishonor. He would disobey the Empress and kill the scum who had the temerity to think that he'd killed the Super-Skrull. The Empress would be furious with K'lrt's impertinence and surely order his execution. K'lrt found that thought reassuring. At least that way he would be able to die as a warrior.

K'lrt soon found the starship captain and destroyed his ship, then dragged the captain out of the wreckage and into the airless void. The Super-Skrull laughed as the captain slowly suffocated in the vacuum of space. His honor restored, K'lrt returned to the new Skrull Throneworld.

But the repercussions of his disobedience were far from what K'lrt had expected.

Although enraged by K'lrt's actions, the Empress did not have him executed. She chose to strip him of his rank. He was forced to become one of the Empress's assassins—a killer striking from the darkness, not allowed to face his victims and give them a chance to die like men. It was a terrible fall from grace for a proud warrior who had once commanded entire armies.

Dorrek would have been pleased.

In his darkened hotel room, K'lrt gnashed his teeth. The sound was like two pieces of sandpaper rubbing together.

"Humans," he spat. "Always has it been the accursed humans who have hounded me, humiliated me, made me a laughingstock throughout the Empire! Always have they kept me from my goals, destroyed my hopes! Always have they kept me from the power that should rightfully be mine—the power to rule the Empire and restore it to its former glory!" He leaped to his feet, his voice rising in anger. *"No more!!"*

All the anger, all the shame K'lrt had suffered over the years, surged through his massive body with the heat of a blazing sun. Storming to the door, he ripped it off its hinges, shattering the withered wood against a wall. If other guests of the hotel heard this disturbance, they wisely kept to their rooms.

K'lrt stomped through the dark hallways to the stairwell that led to the roof and raced upward, taking the steps three at a time. He did not bother shifting his shape to a human form. Swatting aside the thin metal door at the top of the stairwell, he stepped onto a layer of cracked, peeling tar paper. From his vantage point, he glared at the lights of Manhattan.

K'lrt raised his arms high and screamed, a low, bass note that sounded like the howl of a lost soul.

"I am K'lrt!" he bellowed to the stars. *"I am the Super-Skrull, the greatest warrior in the Empire, not some lowly skulker! I will not hide, will not run, any longer!"* He shook his fist at the city. "I *will* kill you, Whitmore! In the name of Sl'gur't, I *swear* you will die this night! But I will not strike at you from the shadows! We will meet face-to-face, as warriors!"

K'lrt's eyes flashed with anger. "And should any 'super heroes' interfere, I will destroy them as well, or die in the attempt! I no longer fear death, Whitmore—my place in Val'kla'mor will be secure, for I shall go to the Eternal Battle as a true Skrull warrior!" A malevolent smile spread across K'lrt's face. "Should I die tonight, it will be with my eyes open, with the honor of the Skrull beating in my heart . . . and with your lifeless corpse in my hands!"

CHAPTER

—7—

"**S**omebody," said Spider-Man, "should be charging admission for this kind of show."

Perched on a lamppost on the corner of Sixth Avenue and Fiftieth Street, the web-slinger looked down to the Hulk, who was leaning casually against a red-white-and-blue mailbox. So far, the strain of supporting the Hulk's considerable weight had only succeeded in snapping two of the bolts that held the mailbox to the sidewalk.

The two heroes watched with amusement as wide-eyed tourists gathered in multitudes to watch a SAFE troop-transport as it hovered above the traffic clogging the avenue. The black-clad agents who had accompanied Spidey and the Hulk on the Skrull chase were moving as quickly as possible to force the crowds back and clear a landing area for the craft.

Major Nefertiti Jones turned to one of her agents—a man in his late thirties, with a sandy-colored mustache and a severe buzz-cut. Jones gestured toward the pressing throngs of onlookers. "Sergeant White, move these people out of the way!"

"Yes, ma'am!" White snapped off a quick salute and trotted off to help the other agents.

Stepping under the Radio City Music Hall marquee, Jones walked up to the sedated Skrull spy, who was still wrapped in Spider-Man's webbing and held tightly by two of Jones's men. Bound as he was, Durklan looked like some sort of space-age mummy topped off by a green, bat-eared head. Agent Montenegro—the sedative-ray generator held tightly in one hand—remained close to Durklan, watching his every move in case he should try to escape.

"Your ride's here," Jones said to the Skrull. Durklan nodded passively. Having been defeated, captured, threatened by the Hulk with bodily harm, and thoroughly sedated, the shapeshifter had offered no further resistance. With little prodding, Durklan had provided his captors with the Super-Skrull's location, then fallen silent.

Around Jones, a constant barrage of camera flashes illuminated the scene of barely-controlled chaos. The lights produced a strobing effect, creating an illusion similar to watching old, scratchy film footage. Gritting her teeth, Jones glared at the would-be paparazzi. There were just too many cameras in use, and far too few agents to seize them all.

"Smile, Major!" Spider-Man called down to Jones. "You're on *Candid Camera!*"

Jones sneered at the wall-crawler. The Hulk chuckled softly.

With a hiss of braking jets, the armored carrier settled to the pavement in front of the Music Hall, neatly parking at the curb. As the entrance ramp lowered from the vehicle, Jones motioned to her agents. Durklan was quickly marched into the transport. The other agents pulled back from their crowd control positions and filed in after the prisoner.

Bringing up the rear, Jones paused in the transport's doorway and turned to the two heroes. "We're taking him back to the hotel. What are you two up to?"

"Well," said the Hulk, "now that we know your prisoner's been secured, we're going to go look up an old . . . acquaintance." He cracked his knuckles and smiled wickedly. "We have a bit of . . . catching-up to do."

Jones frowned. "I'm sure the mayor will appreciate the resulting property damage. Look, I'll have a strike team assembled in minutes and we'll join you at the Super-Skrull's hideout—that is, of course, if the address this spy gave us is accurate. Just try not to level any historical landmarks before we arrive, all right?"

"I make no promises," the Hulk said matter-of-factly. "Like the saying goes, 'to make an omelette, sometimes you have to break a few eggs.' The same goes for mopping up the floor with one of these egomaniacal villains. Sometimes buildings get in the way."

Jones glared at the Hulk. "Don't make me angry, Doctor Banner," she warned. "You've already got enough government agencies looking for your head on a platter—you don't want to add SAFE to the list. Now, I appreciate all you're doing to help us with this problem, and I'm sure Colonel Morgan would be willing to put in a good word for you with the President after we're done." Her lips pulled back in a feral snarl, exposing gleaming white teeth. "But if you cross *me*, you'll wish you'd never been born."

The Hulk waved a hand in a dismissive gesture. He wasn't impressed. "I've heard that before, Major, and from people with a higher rank than yours. I'm still around."

Jones and the Hulk locked gazes, the heat from their respective stares almost visible. Then Jones turned on her heel and stepped into the transport. The door *clanged* shut, and the vehicle rose into the air.

"Nice working with you again, Major!" Spidey yelled at the departing flight. His shout could barely be heard above the roar of manuevering jets.

Spider-Man and the Hulk watched as the carrier rotated and headed back in the direction of the Platinum Towers Hotel. The web-slinger looked at the green-skinned scientist and shook his head. "You've got a real winning way with folks, Doc."

"I can't help it," replied the Hulk. "I'm a 'people' person." He began heading west, toward the Hudson River. "Come on. If we move over to the river and away from the more populated streets, I can jump down to Twenty-ninth Street and cover the distance in no time at all." His eyes narrowed, his lips formed a thin line. "And then, it's payback time."

"Right behind you, Doc," said Spider-Man. Firing a web-line to the cornice of a nearby building, he swung after the jade giant.

The troop-transport landed in front of the Platinum Towers Hotel. Betty and Whitmore—followed closely by their security guards—jogged out of the building just as the carrier's engines shut down. Jones and Elf-man stepped from the vehicle to greet them.

"Is everything all right, Major?" asked Betty. "Where's Bruce?"

"Your husband is fine, Mrs. Banner," said Jones. "Just a bit . . . *trying* at times."

Betty nodded in understanding. "He has that effect on most people."

Whitmore stepped forward. "So, how went your fox hunt, Major? We heard the shots all the way down here. Your men a little quick on the trigger again?"

Jones closed her eyes for a moment and inhaled sharply. It was clear that she was fighting down a wave of anger that threatened to make her say something she would later regret. Slowly exhaling, Jones relaxed and opened her eyes. She tried to put on a friendly smile for Whitmore, but it came out looking more like a sneer.

"For your information, *Mister* Whitmore," Jones said slowly, "my men never fired a shot at the prisoner. What you heard was the very loud report of *his* gun . . . *alone*. And *no* civilians were harmed during the capture."

Now, Whitmore relaxed. *His* smile was much more reassuring. "Well done, Major. Were I wearing a hat, I'd certainly take it off to you."

Betty looked at the transport. "You captured him? Was it the Super-Skrull?"

Jones shook her head. "Unfortunately, no. The one we caught was just a spy, sent to keep an eye on Mr. Whitmore."

Whitmore snorted. "Skrull spies, Skrull assassins . . . my fan club is getting bigger with every passing moment." He looked at Jones. "So, what are you going to do now, Major?"

Jones gestured toward the carrier. "The prisoner has provided us with the Super-Skrull's location. Spider-Man and Doctor Banner have already started on their way there, and we're to meet them before matters get out of hand." She swept her hands toward Betty and Whitmore in a shooing gesture. "Now, if you'll excuse me, I have a strike team to assemble, and not a lot of time to do it in."

"Is there anything I can do to help?" asked Betty.

"Just let us do our job, Mrs. Banner," replied Jones. She turned to the agents still inside the transport. "White and Montenegro! Take Ackerman and Landis and escort the prisoner to the helicarrier for a full de-briefing—I'm sure the Colonel will want to know if the Skrulls are planning any more surprises." She gestured to Elfman. "Elfman! Get the others suited up and ready to move—full-body armor, plasma rifles, concussion charges. We're not taking any chances with this one." Elfman saluted and raced off to assemble the agents.

Jones turned to Betty and Whitmore. "I'm going to need all the operatives I can get for this mission, but I'll leave a pair of agents behind to insure your safety. For all we know, the Skrulls might have a back-up plan ready in case we capture the Super-Skrull."

"And if your men are unable to stop the Super-Skrull?" asked Whitmore.

Jones's lips drew together in a thin line. She looked at Whitmore, but said nothing. The author nodded in understanding.

"I see," he said grimly. "Then I'm a dead man."

* * *

The tangy scent of incense filled the air of the dingy hotel room. K'lrt sat cross-legged on the floor as he prepared for battle. He bowed before a small jade statue of the war god S'glur't. The Super-Skrull muttered softly in his native language, repeating a prayer once taught to him by his father, one passed down through the generations. It was an invocation for S'glur't to give the Skrull the strength to defeat his enemies, or die as a true warrior. And should it be K'lrt's fate to die this night, he asked the war god to permit him passage to Val'kla'mor so that he could join his fallen comrades in the Eternal Battle.

A tremor ran through the building—a small one, almost imperceptible to the ear, but one clearly heard by the Super-Skrull. It was followed by another, then another, each tremor growing in strength until the building was almost vibrating like a tuning fork.

Something was approaching. Something large and powerful.

K'lrt unfolded his legs and slowly rose to his feet. He casually smoothed out the creases in his dark uniform. Then, hands clasped, he bowed to the small statue. K'lrt picked up the idol, wrapped it in a protective cloth, and stored it away in a pouch built into the interior of the metal suitcase that lay on the bed. He looked at the weapons packed away in the valise— blasters, poison darts, intricately designed knives of all shapes and sizes. The tools of an assassin.

The Super-Skrull shook his head. He would not need these. He was a warrior—the greatest warrior in the history of the Empire—and he would die as one.

With a final *thoom!* that shattered the windows in the room, the approaching object came to rest just outside the building. The hotel swayed violently, but K'lrt remained on his feet.

From the hallway, the sounds of screams and running feet drifted into the Super-Skrull's room. The tenants were in a panic, running in all directions. Someone was shouting that the neighborhood was being bombed. The warrior chuckled. How easy it was to upset these humans!

He knew that the vibrations were not caused by explosions. Somehow, his enemies had found him. But the Super-Skrull was not bothered by this revelation—he merely accepted it.

K'lrt smiled.

It was a good day to die.

Spider-Man hung upside-down from a web attached to the underside of the West Side Highway. He gazed at the run-down hotel in front of him, its battered neon sign swaying from the ripples of a shock wave. He looked at the Hulk, who stood in the midst of a crater created by the green behemoth's rough landing. Cracked and broken cobblestones lay scattered in a ring around the Hulk, and the cool night air seemed to vibrate with the echoes of his impact. Tenants—some half-dressed—streamed out of the hotel, practically falling over themselves as they fled. They stampeded around a far corner of the block, ignoring the two super heroes right in front of them. Within a few brief moments, Spidey and the Hulk found themselves alone on an empty street.

The Hulk scratched his head. "*This* is where the Super-Skrull is supposed to be hiding?" he asked increduously.

"That's what the man told us," said Spider-Man. "Kind of a let-down, don't you think? I was expecting him to be holed up in some lavish penthouse. At the very least an underground base that looked like something out of a James Bond movie."

The Hulk shrugged. "Maybe it turns into a spaceship when you push a button."

"Huh," said Spidey. "I guess that spy was serious when he said the Super-Skrull had fallen out of favor with the Empress."

"Good," the Hulk said. "That means they won't have to spend a lot of money on an expensive funeral after I'm through with him. He should fit really well into a matchbox."

"You know, Doc," said Spidey, "I think I liked it better when you used to just say you'd 'smash' somebody. It didn't sound quite so mean-spirited."

"You have a problem with the way I talk, Spider-Man?" asked the Hulk. From his tone of voice, he made the question sound more like a challenge.

I really don't need this kind of hassle, thought Spidey. *Bad enough I'm going to fight somebody who has all of the Fantastic Four's powers. I don't need the Hulk turning against me on top of that.*

"Uh, no, Doc," Spidey said. "Just making a comment."

"Good," murmured the Hulk. He strode toward the building. "Let's get to work."

"Doc! Look out!" yelled Spidey as his spider-sense sent a strong jolt through his body.

Before the Hulk could respond to the warning, a massive fireball exploded against his chest. Knocked off his feet by the impact, the jade giant was thrown to the other side of the street, where he slammed into the side of a car parked at the curb. Unharmed by the flames, the Hulk beat at the fire as it burned away his shirt.

"Blast," rumbled the Hulk. "This was my last good suit."

Following the path of the fireball to its point of origin, Spidey looked up to the roof of the hotel. The Super-Skrull stood there, his upper body awash in flame. He'd activated his Human Torch powers.

"Fools!" bellowed the warrior. "Did you think to catch me unawares?"

"That was the general idea, Skrully," said Spidey. "After all, what good is a surprise party if the guest of honor knows it's coming?" He wagged a disapproving finger at the Skrull. "No cake and ice cream for *you.*"

"But I've got plenty of *punch* to serve!" yelled the Hulk. Stripping off his burned shirt, he stood in the middle of the street, bare-chested and angry.

"Ow," commented Spidey. "And people think *my* puns are bad."

Using his mighty leg muscles, the Hulk propelled himself straight up at the top floor. His momentum carried him over the edge of the roof and straight into the Super-Skrull. They slammed together in a tangle of arms and legs.

"Hang on, Doc!" yelled Spidey. "The cavalry's on the way!" Triggering one of his web-shooters, he fired a line at a billboard and swung over to the hotel, then wall-crawled his way up to the roof. Jumping onto the worn tar paper covering, he came to a halt, momentarily stunned by the sight before him.

The Hulk and Super-Skrull were locked in a deadly struggle. Both combatants were oblivious to his presence. The Hulk's hands were wrapped around the throat of the Skrull, who was ablaze from head to waist. The alien's arms—which appeared to be made of elastic—were entwined around the Hulk's neck and chest in an attempt to strangle and crush him. Spider-Man was reminded of a television nature show he'd once watched, where a python had wrapped itself around its victim, crushing it in the embrace of its deadly coils before devouring it whole.

"What's the matter, frog-face?" croaked the Hulk. "Not going to turn into an old man this time and try to beat me with your cane?"

"Earth scum!" hissed the alien warrior. "I have no need for subterfuge! When you die, I want all to know that it was at the hands of the Super-Skrull!"

"I'll be sure to have those words carved on your tombstone," gasped the Hulk. He shifted his grip on the Skrull's throat, trying to find a better place to grasp.

The Skrull said nothing as he and the Hulk staggered back and forth across the roof, locked in an embrace of strangleholds. To Spider-Man, it looked as though the fighters were performing a bizarre dance number.

I must be nuts, thought Spidey. *I've walked into a regular War of the Gargantuas. Either one of these guys is capable of dropping a house on me, and I'm thinking about getting into the middle of it?* He sighed heavily. *Well, I hope Mary Jane's got a fresh supply of bandages and aspirin at home 'cause, one way or another, this is gonna hurt.*

From a running start, Spider-Man flipped across the roof, somersaulted in mid-air, and launched himself at the Super-Skrull's legs. Slamming into the warrior was like crashing into a brick wall. Spidey's attempt at a flying tackle failed to move the Skrull even an inch, but it did succeed in momentarily distracting him. As K'lrt glanced down to see what had struck him, the Hulk drew back a fist and delivered a staggering uppercut to the Skrull's flaming jaw.

K'lrt reeled back, and the flames covering his upper body sputtered out. His grip on the Hulk loosened and he retracted his arms, shifting them back to their normal size and shape. The Skrull shook his head to clear it.

But Spider-Man knew better than to give the Super-Skrull an opportunity to catch his breath. Leaping forward, he drove his feet into K'lrt's stomach. The warrior gasped, the air driven from his lungs. Spidey quickly encased the dazed alien in a thick layer of webbing. Unable to retain his balance, K'lrt crashed to the surface of the roof and lay there, stunned.

"Nice packaging," the Hulk said to Spidey.

"Thanks," said Spidey. "I'm a whiz with Christmas presents." He nodded toward the Skrull. "That's not gonna hold him for long, you know."

"Leave that to me," the Hulk said, grinning mirthlessly. He stomped toward the Super-Skrull—

—*just as the wall-crawler's spider-sense flashed a warning!*

"Get back!" Spidey yelled.

The Super-Skrull seemed to explode in a huge fireball, the heat of the blast driving the two heroes to the far side of the roof. The layer of cheap tar paper under

Spider-Man knew better than to give the Super-Skrull an opportunity to catch his breath.

their feet melted, adding fuel to the fire. In seconds, the roof had become a raging inferno. Spidey and the Hulk soon found themselves pushed into a corner.

"Well, this is going just swimmingly," Spider-Man said sarcastically. "For a second there, I'd actually convinced myself this was gonna be an easy fight!"

"Get out of here, Spider-Man!" said the Hulk. "The fire can't harm me, but you don't have any kind of protection."

"Nothing doing, Doc!" replied Spidey. "What kind of a friendly, neighborhood Spider-Man would I be if I were afraid of a little fire? I've got a reputation to uphold, you know!" He pointed toward the center of the roof. "Besides, I think Round Two's about to start!"

Through the heart of the blaze walked the Super-Skrull. The hatred in his eyes burned as brightly as the flames around him. His unique powers had protected him from the fire.

"Cretins!" he yelled. "You think the greatest Skrull warrior of all could be defeated by a few blows?"

"I don't know," said Spidey. "I'll have to ask him when he gets here."

K'lrt gnashed his teeth and growled. His eyes seem to glow with an unnatural light as he glared at the web-spinner.

And then something unseen smashed into Spidey's head with the speed of a bullet train. He staggered to the edge of the roof.

"Spider-Man!" cried the Hulk. The jade giant spun quickly, trying to grab hold of the wall-crawler, but it was too late. Spider-Man toppled over the side.

Before the green behemoth could leap after Spider-

Man, a rock-hard fist crashed into his jaw, quickly followed by a crushing blow to his forehead. Dazed by the combination of punches, the Hulk dropped to one knee. He swallowed, tasting blood. More blood seeped from a nasty cut on his head.

The Hulk looked up to find K'lrt standing nearby. The warrior's hands were transformed into large, lumpy fists that looked as though they had been carved from orange stone. Normally, such hands were found only on the Thing, the strongest member of the Fantastic Four. However, K'lrt's powers allowed him to mimic the Thing's strength and his unique physical attributes.

"You have been a worthy opponent, Hulk," said the Super-Skrull. "A true warrior. I promise to make your death a quick one. Then, I will complete my mission and dispose of your friend Whitmore." He chuckled softly. "I am certain the Empress will think better of me once I have presented to her a very special gift: the corpses of two enemies of the Skrull Empire."

The Hulk sneered. "You're just full of yourself, aren't you? Well, I've got just the thing to cure you of *that* problem."

With an inhuman roar, he launched himself at the Skrull. The two combatants flew over the roof and plummeted toward the street.

On the other side of the building, two stories down, Spider-Man slowly came to his senses. His back was sore, and his right arm was raised above his head. Spidey looked up at his arm to see he was grasping a web-line that was adhered to a window ledge one story above him. Below him, his feet swung freely over the deserted street.

Now I remember, thought Spidey. *Managed to fire out a web-line while I was falling, but then I slammed into the building. Knocked me for a loop.* He rubbed his head. *Super-Skrull must've been using the Invisible Woman's powers—hit me with some kind of invisible bludgeon.* Releasing the web-line, he clung to the side of the building and rubbed his stiff shoulder. *Wonder how the Doc is doing?*

A sudden ear-shattering *boom!* that rocked the street gave the wall-crawler some idea of what was going on. The building swayed dangerously as a powerful tremor ran through it. In a shower of sparks, the hotel sign broke loose from its supports and crashed down onto the sidewalk. Bricks dislodged from the front of the building. Windows shattered.

"I think this little wall-crawler better find a safer place to cling to!" Spidey said to himself. He leaped from the wall, firing a web-line to the West Side Highway overpass, and swung over to the metal structure. From there, he shot another line to a lamppost, swinging from the roadway to the far side of the hotel to find the source of the minor earthquake.

It looked as though a meteorite had struck lower Manhattan. A massive crater sank deep into the cobblestoned street, the result of the impact created by the Hulk and Super-Skrull when they had fallen from the roof. Spider-Man could see damaged telephone cables and a cracked water main, the latter spewing out a steady stream of liquid. There were other broken pipes, but Spidey couldn't identify them, or the purpose they served.

His attention was drawn to the end of the block. The Hulk and Super-Skrull were once more trading blows. The green-skinned scientist had taken to using parked cars as weapons, tossing them at the alien warrior.

"Not so much fun when *you're* the one getting three-thousand pounds of Detroit steel thrown in your face, is it?" said the Hulk.

"Bah!" barked the Skrull, effortlessly batting away a minivan. "You merely delay the inevitable! Whitmore *will* die before this night is over, but not before I have crushed your skull like a ripe melon!"

"Hey, Skrully!" yelled Spider-Man, swinging over to join the confrontation. He landed beside the Hulk. "I don't know about you, but all this talk of melons is making me hungry. What do you say we stop all this fighting and just go grocery shopping? You can show me how to pick out the ripe ones. Is there some trick to doing it?"

"I tire of your ceaseless banter, Spider-Man," growled the Skrull. "Rest assured, when I am done with the Hulk, you shall be the next to—"

A glob of webbing struck K'lrt's face, covering it completely. He roared in anger and pulled at the adhesive.

"Oh, how you *do* go on!" said Spidey, in a fair imitation of Bugs Bunny. He watched the Skrull tearing at the webbing. "Uh, I wouldn't do that if I were you, Skrully," he said in his normal voice. "That stuff stays stuck for an hour and it could—"

With a scream of anguish, K'lrt tore the webbing from his face, ripping away a layer of skin. Dark green fluid streamed down his features, painting Skrull-blood stripes from temple to chin. It reminded Spider-Man of a tribal war mask.

Before he could make a quip about the Super-Skrull's new look, Spider-Man suddenly fell silent, then began sniffing the air. He turned to the Hulk. "Hey, Doc, do you smell—"

"EVERYONE STAY WHERE YOU ARE!" commanded a female voice.

The three fighters looked up to see the SAFE troop-transport hovering above the street. In the forward cab sat Major Jones and another agent. Jones had been talking through the loudspeaker mounted on the roof of the vehicle.

With a blast of landing jets, the carrier descended on the far side of the crater, behind Spider-Man and the Hulk. The doors opened and, weapons at the ready, the SAFE strike team poured out to take positions along the street. Dressed like her troops, in gleaming black body armor, Jones stepped forward to stand beside the two heroes. In one hand she held a plasma rifle. Roughly the same size and shape of a military-issue weapon, the rifle fired not bullets, but a beam of highly charged particles of superheated gas.

"Super-Skrull!" said Jones, pointing to the alien. "My name is Major Jones. I am ordering you to surrender. Lie on the ground with your hands clasped firmly behind your head. Failure to comply with this order will be met with hostile force!"

The Super-Skrull stared at Jones for a moment, then laughed.

"Well, that didn't have the desired effect," Spidey muttered softly. Jones slowly turned her head to glare at him.

"I have an order for *you*, woman!" shouted the warrior. "Stand aside so that I may complete my mission.

Should you refuse, neither you nor your men will leave this place alive."

"He's a real charmer, isn't he?" murmured Jones to Spider-Man. The web-slinger opted to remain silent, and nodded his agreement. Gripping the weapon with both hands, Jones hefted the plasma rifle to shoulder-level and aimed the barrel at the Skrull. The plasma generator whined as it built-up a charge.

"I'm afraid I can't do that," Jones told the Super-Skrull.

K'lrt nodded. "As I expected." His hands shimmered, changing from orange rock to crackling flame.

Seeing the fire brought Spider-Man's thoughts back to the broken pipes in the crater, and the unusual smell he'd detected. He looked back at the hole, trying to think of what those pipes might contain. Then the realization hit him: *they were gas lines.*

Spider-Man turned to the Super-Skrull, waving frantically at the alien. "NO!" he cried. "Don't do it!"

The next few moments seemed to pass in slow motion for Spider-Man. He saw the Super-Skrull extend his arms, which glowed with the brightness of a sun. Major Jones and her men leveled their weapons at the alien, preparing to fire. The Hulk lunged forward to attack his foe. A blast of flame erupted from the Skrull's hands. Spider-Man scooped Jones into his arms and leaped across the street, aiming for a window facing onto the Lansdale Hotel lobby.

And then the world exploded around them.

CHAPTER
—8—

From the windows of Berkley Whitmore's room on the twenty-first floor of the Platinum Towers Hotel, Betty Banner watched in horror as a massive fireball blossomed above the streets of lower Manhattan. For a moment, the deep blue evening skies were splashed with bright red—the color of freshly spilled blood. The explosion's shockwave struck the hotel seconds later, violently rattling the glass panes.

Visibly shaken, Betty nervously chewed on a thumb nail. She stared, transfixed, as the fireball expended its energy and began to dissipate. In its place rose a thick column of smoke that blotted out the stars overhead and covered the city in a black shroud.

"Bruce," Betty whispered.

Whitmore raced out from the bathroom. "What in blazes was that?" he asked. Seeing Betty frozen in place, he joined her at the window and put a hand on her shoulder. "Betty?" he said softly.

Betty said nothing, continuing to gaze through the

glass. Whitmore followed the direction of her wide-eyed stare and spotted the blaze to the south.

"Good Lord," he murmured.

Still in a trance, Betty turned to Whitmore. She looked as though she had just realized he was standing beside her. Betty shook her head to clear it. "Berk, I . . . I've got to go. I have to see if Bruce is okay."

Whitmore gave her a reassuring smile and patted her on the shoulder. "I understand. And I'm going with you."

"No, Berk!" Betty objected. "In case you've forgotten, the Super-Skrull is trying to *kill* you. The last thing you should do is make his job easier by going to him!"

"I appreciate the concern, Betty," said Whitmore, "but I've never been comfortable with people fighting my battles for me—*even* if the guy looking to punch out my lights is a lantern-jawed lummox from another planet." He gave her a friendly tap on the chin with his knuckles. "Besides, kiddo, who's gonna watch *your* back with all those trigger-happy whackos shooting at each other?"

Betty smiled weakly. "There's no way I'm going to convince you to change your mind, is there?"

Whitmore gestured toward the firearm Betty carried in her shoulder holster. "Not unless you plan on waving that thing in my face." He drew himself up to his full height and folded his arms across his chest. "And I wouldn't try that if I were you."

Betty nodded. "All right. But how do we get down there?"

One of Whitmore's eyebrows rose. The look on his face was similar to that of a teacher hearing a student give him a half-baked excuse about not turning in a homework assignment. "Hadn't you taken that into consideration?"

"Look, Berk," said Betty. "I just witnessed a huge explosion in the direction we saw the SAFE agents headed. Knowing my husband, he was probably at Ground Zero when the blast happened. My first reaction was to see if he's alive, not take the time to think things out." She ran a hand through her fiery hair and exhaled sharply. "I'm kind'a running purely on adrenaline right now, you know?"

Whitmore nodded, then thought for a moment. "Well, I saw some SAFE hovercraft parked in the street. We could 'borrow' one and fly to the scene. You have any experience with those space-age flivvers?"

"Sure, I can handle one," said Betty. "But I'll need a key or a pilot's access code in order to start-up its engine."

"That's not a problem," assured Whitmore. "If we can't find a starter key for it, I can always hotwire the thing."

Betty looked stunned by this news. "Now, how would you know about hotwiring an engine? Bruce never mentioned you doing anything like that."

Whitmore winked at Betty and smiled. "Bruce doesn't know everything about me, kiddo. Just chalk up this particular talent of mine to my misspent days as a youth." He headed for the door. "Come on. Let's go check on your hubby."

It looked as though hell had opened a franchise in downtown Manhattan.

Fires raged out of control, fueled by ruptured gas

mains and sparking power lines. The moans of the injured, the terrified, and the dying echoed through the streets. The air was thick and black with the stench of burning rubber as car tires melted under the withering heat. The ear-piercing shriek of approaching sirens sounded like a mournful wail.

The Lansdale Hotel and surrounding buildings were engulfed in flame. Windows for blocks around were shattered. Cobblestones sent rocketing through the air by the force of the blast lay embedded in walls and vehicles. Some had even been wedged into the side of the West Side Highway. The crater originally created by the Hulk and the Super-Skrull had widened and now filled the entire block. From its center shot a geyser of flame that rose a hundred feet into the air. Around the devastation, residents of the neighborhood fled their apartments, some stumbling around in shock, others clutching whatever possessions they could grab as they ran for their lives.

The lobby of the Lansdale Hotel was shattered. The blast had crumbled its walls into piles of broken plaster bits, splintered the wooden furnishings, and scorched the worn tile floor. On the side of the building that faced the crater, a row of filthy windows had been replaced by a gaping hole, through which debris from the explosion had been catapulted.

And in that debris, something stirred.

In the center of the lobby, covered in plaster dust, lay a sagging gray cocoon made of synthetic webbing. With a loud *rip!* the sticky fibers split open to deposit Spider-Man and Major Jones on the warm tiles. They lay on the floor for a few moments, coughing spasmodically. The coughs subsided, and Spider-Man rolled to a sitting position.

"Well," he said hoarsely, *"that's* one experience I'd just as soon never repeat."

Jones propped herself up on one elbow. She unclipped the chin-straps of her combat helmet and let the metal headpiece drop to the floor. "I'm getting too old for this stuff," she rasped. Jones looked back at the hole in the wall, then turned to Spider-Man. "If you hadn't carried us through that window—"

"When there used to be a window there," interjected Spidey.

"—I'd hate to think what would've happened to us," Jones finished. "Thank you."

Spider-Man unsteadily rose to his feet. "Always glad to be of service, Major." He picked a smoky piece of webbing off his costume. "No extra charge for the fire blanket."

Jones nodded, then picked up her helmet. "Let's see what's been happening out there." She thumbed a switch inside the headpiece. "Elfman, what's our status?" Static poured from the miniature receiver. "Elfman, come back." There was no reply.

"Blast," Jones muttered. She put the helmet back on her head and locked the straps.

Spider-Man lowered a hand to help Jones to her feet, but staggered back before she could grab it.

Jones eyed him carefully. "Are you all right?" she asked, clearly concerned.

"I've felt better," Spidey admitted. He looked down at his torn costume. Through the frayed material, he could see reddened, burned skin. Reaching an arm behind himself, Spidey delicately touched his back. His next breath came out as a ragged hiss of pain.

Using her rifle for support, Jones stood up and walked behind Spider-Man. She gritted her teeth as she spotted the damage done to the wall-crawler's back: The costume's large spider-symbol had been burned away to reveal skin that was raw and bloody. It looked like it had been scraped with a cheese grater.

"You need a doctor," Jones said.

"My back will heal," said Spider-Man. "Trust me. When you've been doing this costumed hero gig for as long as I have, you learn to deal with the pain." He turned to walk toward the hole in the wall, and groaned loudly.

Jones put a hand on his arm to stop him. "You're not going anywhere."

"But the Super-Skrull—"

"Can wait," Jones insisted. "If you want to jump back in there for another round of fisticuffs, fine—I've got your back. But you're not running out of here until we've done something about those injuries." She reached down to a slim pack velcroed to the leg of her armor. "First-aid kit. Whatever I do to fix you up isn't going to heal the burns, but it should reduce the chances for infection."

Spider-Man wearily sat down on the ruins of the front desk. "Fair enough. I leave myself in your capable hands, Major."

Opening the first aid kit, Jones pulled out a bottle of spray disinfectant and set to work on the burns.

Bruce Banner—the incredible Hulk—slowly awoke to find himself in pitch blackness. He groaned, feeling as though a large weight was sitting on his head—which was true. A late model sedan had landed on him, and the rear axle was pressing against his skull. Hoisting himself to his feet, the Hulk tossed the car off his back and looked around.

Fire trucks, police cars, and ambulances were just arriving on the scene at the far end of the block. Paramedics rushed to aid the injured SAFE agents. It appeared that the body armor had managed to protect some of the men. Unfortunately, not all of the agents had been lucky. A trio of them lay broken and bloodied near the edge of the crater.

The Hulk snarled, clearly angered by the sight of the dead men, and looked around. "Where are you, Skrull?" he bellowed. "I know you couldn't have been killed by the explosion, but I'm gonna make you wish you had! Come out and fight! It's time we finished this!"

"I am here, human," said a calm voice beside him.

The Hulk turned, but saw nothing. Then something invisible smashed against his face, breaking his nose. A rapid succession of blows followed, to his face, his ribs, his kidneys. The Hulk staggered back, but the volley continued, hammering him again and again. Blood coated his face like a dark-green mask.

Wildly, the jade giant lashed out, throwing punches in all directions, but he struck only air. "Stop hiding!" the Hulk roared in frustration. "Fight me like a man!"

The Hulk's demand was met with derisive laughter that echoed all around him.

More unseen blows rained down on him. A strike to his temple, disorienting him. Another kidney-punch. A sharp hit to his spine. A double-fisted blow to his stomach, driving the air from his lungs. The Hulk gasped, trying to breathe, but he couldn't draw in any air. Numbly, the green-skinned scientist raised his hands to reach his head, only to meet with resistance. Something was encasing his head, cutting off much-needed oxygen.

The Hulk was suffocating.

He crumpled to his knees, trying to tear off the invisible object, but it remained firmly in place. The Hulk's eyes began glazing over, and his hands dropped to his sides—he was beginning to pass out. Unless he could free himself in the next few minutes, he would die.

Which was the perfect cue for the Super-Skrull to make himself visible. Mimicking the Invisible Woman's powers, he had launched his successful attack against the Hulk, remaining unseen while striking with the Thing's strength. Having sealed the green behemoth's head in an invisible force bubble, it was clear that K'lrt could sense pending victory as he watched his enemy gasp for air.

Spotting the warrior, the Hulk roared, but the sound could not be heard outside the bubble. He pounded on the globe with both fists, each strike more powerful than the one before it, but it was a futile effort. The bubble was unbreakable.

"You have fought well, Hulk," said the Super-Skrull. "I shall always remember you as a valiant opponent. But the time has come for our battle to end. I still have a mission to complete."

K'lrt raised his hands and launched a stream of white-hot flame at the Hulk. Unable to breathe or escape, the jade giant writhed like a fish caught on a hook. His cries of agony were swallowed by the force bubble.

A roar of jets from behind K'lrt warned him that something was approaching, fast. He turned to see the source of the disturbance—

—and was slammed in the back by a SAFE hover-craft that struck with the force of a missile.

In the lobby of the Lansdale Hotel, Spider-Man and Major Jones heard the Hulk's shouts for the Super-Skrull to reveal himself, followed by the sounds of combat.

"Come on, Major," Spidey said impatiently. "I can't leave the Doc out there alone to take on the Skrull."

"Look, Spider-Man," said Jones, "the choice is simple. Either you let me dress your wounds properly, or I shoot you in the knee to insure you don't become a liability in this fight. I won't have my men put at risk just because you wanted to prove what a tough guy you are, only to fold up when they needed you the most."

Applying the last of her kit's bandages to the wall-crawler's back, Jones taped them in place with strips of webbing that Spidey had provided. "All right, I'm done," she said. "You sure it won't hurt when this webbing has to be taken off?" she asked.

"It'll dissolve in an hour," replied Spidey, standing up. "In the meantime, it'll hold the bandages in place much better than any surgical tape." He straightened his back, then rolled his head to loosen his shoulder muscles. "Almost as good as new. Thanks, Major."

Jones smiled. "Anytime, masked man."

Spider-Man removed a pair of small cartridges from

his web-shooters, replacing them with a fresh set from a belt under his costume. "Okay," he said. "We're good to go. Now, let's go bag us a Skrull."

Picking their way through the rubble, Spidey and Jones stepped from the hotel in time to see the Super-Skrull get run down by the hovercraft. The impact tossed the warrior high into the night sky. The flying vehicle continued down the length of the block, then banked sharply, headed back, and struck the alien again as he fell. Caught totally unaware, the Skrull had no time to activate his Fantastic Four powers. Betty's surprise attack did the trick. K'lrt was unconscious before he hit the ground. He toppled head over heels and slammed into the pavement face-first. He laid there, not moving.

"Ow," commented Spidey. "You *know* that's gotta hurt."

With a roar of jets, the hovercraft wobbled to a near-perfect landing, and settled to the ground beside the Hulk. The jade giant was kneeling, drawing great lungfuls of air into his massive body. Betty leaped from the vehicle and ran to her husband.

"Bruce! Bruce! What's wrong?" Betty frantically asked.

"Nothing . . . now," croaked the Hulk. "Lousy Skrull was trying to suffocate me. When you ran over him, he lost control of his invisible powers, and the bubble he had around my head dissolved." He gave Betty a peck on the cheek. "Thanks, honey."

Jones looked from the happy couple to the emergency units gathered down the street. She breathed a sigh of relief when she spotted Elfman supervising the medical aid being provided for injured SAFE agents.

Jones turned to Spider-Man. "I've got to check on my men. But from what I see, it's pretty clear we're out of this fight. It's up to you and Doctor Banner now. Find some way to restrain the Skrull before he becomes a problem again. And do it fast, before he wakes up." She headed for the nearest ambulance.

"You've got it, Major!" said Spidey. He gave a quick salute and ran to take care of the Super-Skrull.

"Is it safe—pardon my unintentional pun—to come out now?" asked Whitmore, climbing from the hover-craft. The winds generated by his and Betty's wild aerial ride across Manhattan had transformed Whitmore's wild mane of copper hair into the kind of fright wig normally seen on the bride of Frankenstein.

"Berk, are you crazy?" said the Hulk, slowly standing with Betty's help. "You shouldn't be here!" He looked to his wife. "Betty—"

"Don't blame Betty, Bruce," Whitmore said sternly. "I forced her to bring me along. You didn't think I was going to let my best friend's wife run into the middle of a battlefield alone, did you?"

"But, Berk," said the Hulk, "what's the sense in trying to protect you if you're just going to unnecessarily put your neck on the chopping block?"

"You worry too much, Banner," Whitmore said lightheartedly. He pointed with his chin toward the Super-Skrull. Spider-Man was kneeling beside the warrior, binding his arms and legs with thick strands of webbing. "From what I see, you've got the situation under control." Whitmore put an arm around Betty's shoulders and gave her a small squeeze. "You should be proud of Betty, Bruce. It's not often a guy the size of a mountain gets to sit back and let his wife handle the dirty work."

"Still . . ." began the Hulk. Then he shrugged and said, "All right. I guess you can watch, but I want you to do it from somewhere safe." He turned to Betty. "Take the hovercraft up a hundred feet or so and move it to the far end of the block. That should put enough breathing room between you and the Skrull, and still give Berk a good view of what we're doing."

Whitmore happily slapped the Hulk on the arm. "Great! It'll be just like sitting in the upper deck at Yankee Stadium!" He grabbed Betty's wrist and pulled her toward the hovercraft. "Get the lead out, Mrs. Banner—we don't want all the good seats taken!"

With a sigh, Betty allowed Whitmore to drag her into the vehicle.

Halfway down the street, Spider-Man had finished securing the Super-Skrull's arms and legs with webbing. Still kneeling beside the unconscious alien, Spidey checked over his handiwork, then gazed at the warrior's features. K'lrt's lips were still drawn back in a perpetual sneer.

"Now, here's a guy that all the beauty sleep in the world couldn't help," Spidey commented. He turned to the Hulk, who was conversing with Betty and Whitmore by the hovercraft. Spidey was about to call out to the green goliath—

—when his spider-sense shrieked a warning!

Turning around, Spider-Man looked down and found himself staring into the blood-red pupils of the Super-Skrull. The warrior's eyes seemed to grow larger, their gaze boring deep into the web-slinger's mind. Spider-Man tried to turn his head to tear himself away from that hypnotic stare, but it was too late. He opened his mouth, tried to shout out a warning to the Hulk, but the only sound that escaped his lips was a soft groan. His arms felt like lead weights, and they dropped heavily by his sides.

"Your mind belongs to me, human," murmured the Skrull, his voice no louder than a soft rumble. "Cease your struggles. Your limited intellect is no match for my superior hypnotic abilities."

K'lrt raised himself to a sitting position. He growled softly as he caught sight of Whitmore settling into the hovercraft's passenger seat. "Of course. It was inevitable that he would come. It is always the coward's way to gloat over an enemy when he has been vanquished by others."

Flexing his powerful muscles, the Skrull snapped his web restraints and smiled grimly. "Now that all the actors have been assembled on-stage, the time has come for the final act." He turned to Spider-Man, who remained unmoving. "As for *you* . . ."

A rock-hard fist smashed into Spider-Man's head and the hero fell hard.

The Super-Skrull activated his invisibilty power and ran toward the hovercraft.

"Now, listen," the Hulk said to Betty as he leaned against the driver's side of the craft. "If there's any kind of trouble—however slight it may appear—I want you to get out of here and take Berk somewhere safe. Try Avengers Mansion or the FF's headquarters. If they're both out of town, find out where the SAFE helicarrier is and take him there. Hopefully, that shouldn't be necessary. I think Spider-Man is just about finished wi—"

The Hulk stopped as he looked over toward Spider-Man. The web-slinger was lying on the pavement, apparently unconscious. Beside him was a small mound of torn webbing.

But there was no sign of the Super-Skrull.

"Betty!" the Hulk exclaimed. "The Skrull's loose! Get Berk out of—"

A powerful, unseen uppercut tagged the Hulk on his jaw. The jade giant's head viciously snapped back. Two more swift blows and he collapsed, semi-conscious, on the pavement.

Betty threw the hovercraft into gear. The vehicle started to lift off just as the Super-Skrull made himself visible. He was standing right beside the driver's side. The warrior grabbed the front of the craft with both hands and overturned it, spilling Betty and Whitmore onto the street. K'lrt swung the vehicle like a baseball bat and swatted the dazed Hulk into the smoking remains of the Lansdale Hotel. With a *crash!* the entire building collapsed on the green goliath. The Super-Skrull tossed away the craft and turned back to his target.

Placing herself between Whitmore and K'lrt, Betty unholstered her gun and fired blast after blast at the Skrull. The powerful plasma beams never reached the warrior, impacting instead against an invisible force field that had been erected two feet in front of the alien.

The Super-Skrull glared at Whitmore. "Is this the 'great man' to whom I had considered offering a warrior's death—a coward who lets a *woman* do his fighting for him?" He laughed and gestured toward the author. "Even now, you shake with fear!"

Betty glanced over her shoulder to find Whitmore doubled-over, his body shuddering with terrible spasms. Moving to his side, Betty wrapped her arms around his shoulders to try to stop his shaking. "Berk, what's wrong?"

"It's been . . . so long . . ." Whitmore muttered.

Suddenly, his head and hands shimmered, his facial features blurring and flowing like water. His skin turned a sickly-green color. His ears grew larger and became bat-shaped. His chin became deeply furrowed. Betty's eyes widened in horror as she watched the transformation.

Berkley Whitmore was a Skrull.

Betty gasped. She pushed herself away from Whitmore. "No . . ." she whispered.

The author-turned-alien looked pleadingly at Betty. "Betty, please. I can explain—"

"No!" Betty roared. "I don't want to hear any excuses! Bruce was your friend, someone he thought he could trust! But you never trusted *him*, did you? You never told him who you really are!" She pointed an accusatory finger at Whitmore. "You've been lying to us all along! You *knew* why the Super-Skrull was sent to kill you, but you weren't willing to trust us—your *friends!*—with that knowledge!" Eyes brimming with tears, Betty gazed in apparent anguish at Whitmore. She looked betrayed. *"Why, Berk?"*

Whitmore lowered his head and said nothing.

The Super-Skrull smiled maliciously at Betty. "You did not know? He never told you?" He chuckled. "Ironic, is it not? All this time, and you never realized that you were protecting one of Earth's enemies."

Whitmore, his crimson pupils flashing with anger,

Berkley Whitmore was a Skrull.

glared at the Super-Skrull. Slowly, he stood up to face his would-be killer.

"All right, K'lrt," said Whitmore, "I've listened to enough of your crowing. Are you here to carry out a mission, or do you plan on boring me to death with long-winded speeches that only serve to stroke that over-inflated ego of yours?" The author sneered at the Super-Skrull. "Or is all that talk just your way of building up the courage to kill someone?"

K'lrt growled and gnashed his teeth. "I will take great pleasure in killing *you*."

"Blah, blah, blah," sniped Whitmore. "You're boring me, K'lrt. No wonder you get your butt kicked so often—as a warrior, you make one heck of a speechmaker."

The Super-Skrull roared in anger.

Whitmore quickly turned to Betty. "Get out of here, kid! This is going to get ugly fast!"

Betty seemed frozen by indecision. It was clear that her thoughts were in turmoil. On one hand, she was caught between two Skrulls—members of an alien race that had been trying to conquer Earth for decades. On the other hand, one of those Skrulls was Berkley Whitmore, a man she had grown to admire in the short time they had been together.

Pulling Betty to her feet, Whitmore gave her a forceful shove. *"Go!"*

Raising his arms, the Super-Skrull's hands began glowing with white-hot heat. K'lrt prepared to incinerate his intended victims . . .

. . . Only to be interrupted by Spider-Man landing on his back. The web-slinger delivered two quick punches to the back of the Skrull's neck that sent the alien reeling.

"Hey, watch it with those hands, junior!" Spider-Man said. "We don't know where they've been! I think you'd better go and wash them before you start frying your friends. And while you're at it, better wash your face, too. There's gunk all over it." Triggering his web-shooters, Spidey covered the Skrull's face with a thick glop of adhesive. "Well, *now* there is."

The Skrull bellowed in anger and pulled at the webbing.

Whitmore grabbed Betty's hand. "Come on, kiddo. We're getting out of here." Pulling along his visibly shaken friend, Whitmore headed for the nearest shelter: the abandoned highway overpass.

Suddenly, the Super-Skrull's body roared into flame. Warned by his spider-sense a split-second before the alien caught fire, Spidey leaped away, narrowly avoiding a fresh set of burns. Somersaulting off-balance through the air, Spidey flopped onto the pavement and screamed in pain. The impact had reopened the wounds on his back. He lay on the ground, unable to move, his breath coming out in ragged gasps.

The Super-Skrull burned away the last of the webbing covering his face. He glanced at Spider-Man writhing on the ground and sneered. "Weakling," he muttered.

K'lrt looked around in time to see Betty and Whitmore running under the overpass. Smoothing out the creases in his uniform, the warrior watched with amusement as his prey ran for what they appeared to consider shelter. K'lrt began striding after them.

With a roar like a mountain avalanche, the collapsed

remains of the Lansdale Hotel flew apart, and the Hulk stepped out. His eyes blazed with fury as he glared at the Super-Skrull.

"I'm not finished with you, yet," growled the jade giant. "When somebody drops a building on me, I expect them to stick around so I can return the favor."

"If you insist on dying today, human," said the Super-Skrull, "then I shall be more than willing to accommodate you. First, though, I have a mission to complete."

Before the Hulk could move to stop him, K'lrt hurled a massive fireball at the West Side Highway. Following the path the deadly missile was taking, the green behemoth saw with horror who the intended targets were: his wife and . . . another Skrull?

"Nooo!" the Hulk shouted.

Pushing off with his powerful legs, the Hulk leaped into the air to intercept the fireball, but he was too late. The missile struck the overpass and exploded, shattering the abandoned roadway. Twisted steel beams and pulverized concrete rained down as the overpass collapsed.

And caught in the midst of that deadly shower were Betty Banner and Berkley Whitmore.

CHAPTER
9

"**B**etty!" cried the Hulk.

The jade giant landed beside the mound of debris that used to be the overpass. Frantically, he began tossing aside huge slabs of concrete, digging his way toward the center of the mound.

Behind him, the Super-Skrull roared with laughter and shook a fist at the night sky.

"Are you watching, my Empress?" the alien bellowed triumphantly to the stars. "Do you see how a *warrior* deals with an enemy of the Empire? Not by skulking in the shadows, but by facing his opponent! Letting him see Death as it comes for him!" He thumped his chest with a mighty fist. "At last, my honor is restored! Once more shall K'lrt be hailed as the greatest Skrull of all! Now, not even the Empress can deny me the glory that is rightfully mine!"

The Super-Skrull's chest swelled with pride. Turning his attention to the wrecked overpass, he watched with mild interest as the Hulk continued digging through the rubble. K'lrt sneered. "And now, it is time to make good on a long-standing promise. The Hulk's head will make a fine trophy to present to the Empress." K'lrt strode toward his next intended victim.

Halfway down the street, Spider-Man lay on the smoldering pavement, fighting the waves of mind-numbing pain that swept over him. Slowly, his labored breathing eased as the pain subsided. Cramped muscles relaxing, the web-slinger exhaled sharply and propped himself up on one elbow.

"That's it," he moaned. "I've *gotta* start looking for a real job."

Raising himself to a sitting position, Spider-Man shook his head to clear it. Looking around, he spotted the Super-Skrull closing in on the Hulk. The green behemoth, intent on his search for Betty and Whitmore, was oblivious to the Skrull's advance.

"Betty!" the Hulk yelled. "Can you hear me? Answer me!"

"Oh, no," murmured Spider-Man as he realized what was going on. Unsteadily, he rose to his feet. He gasped as his tender back sent bolts of pain shooting up and down his spine.

I must be outta my mind, Spider-Man thought. *I've got burns over most of my body, I can't take two steps without getting woozy, my head feels like somebody's been whacking it with a mallet all day long, and every muscle I've got feels ready to give out. But despite all that, I'm thinking about locking horns with a bat-eared psycho from outer space who almost managed to take out the* Hulk *a little while ago?* He shook his head. *Mary Jane's never gonna forgive me if I get myself killed. . . .*

The wall-crawler staggered forward, aiming his body in the direction of the Skrull. With each step, he forced himself to increase his pace, until he was moving at a fair gallop. Springing into the air, Spidey shot out a web-line to one of the few lampposts on the block still standing and swung after the alien warrior.

With a monstrous groan of exertion, the Hulk tossed away a slab of concrete and twisted metal bars, finally reaching the center of the mound of debris. A group of steel girders had fallen against one another, forming a rough teepee. The Hulk shoved the beams to one side . . . and stopped as he looked down to find not his wife and the Skrull he had spotted with her, but an oversized green globe.

"What . . . ?" said the Hulk, clearly confused.

On the surface of the globe a seam appeared, which widened to a hole. From the object spilled Betty Banner, dirty and disheveled, but otherwise unhurt. The Hulk kneeled beside his wife as she gratefully drew in deep lungfuls of air.

"Betty . . . ?" the jade giant said softly.

"I'm fine, Bruce," replied Betty. "Just give me a second." She smiled and affectionately patted his cheek.

"Where's Berk?" asked the Hulk. "And where did that other Skrull come from?"

"Other . . . ?" Betty turned from her husband to look at the globe as it changed shape. Within seconds, - it had shifted back to the form of a bat-eared resident of the Skrull Empire.

"Oh," Betty said, almost in a whisper.

The alien coughed, then groaned and rubbed his stiff neck. He looked to the Hulk, who was glaring at him.

"What's the matter, Bruce?" said the Skrull in an all-too-familiar voice. "Never seen a green man before?"

"Berk . . . ?" the Hulk muttered. His jaw went slack as he stared, clearly confused, at his old friend . . . who was now a Skrull.

"Better close that mouth, big guy," Whitmore said good-naturedly, "before you start attracting flies." He looked at Betty. "You all right?"

"Uh . . . yes," said Betty, a little stiffly. "Thank you for saving my life."

"My pleasure," said Whitmore, smiling. "I'd do it again in a heartbeat. After all, I couldn't very well lose one of my closest friends, could I? I have so few of them."

Betty seemed to hesitate for a moment in replying. Then a smile slowly spread across her face. She gently placed a hand on Whitmore's arm. "Thank you, Berk," she said softly.

"I-I don't understand any of this," the Hulk stammered.

"It's a long story, Bruce," said Whitmore. "And one that I'd be more than happy to tell you . . . *later*. Right now, this really isn't the proper time or place for explanations." He gestured over the Hulk's shoulder. "Not when we still have *him* to deal with."

The green-skinned adventurer looked back to see the Super-Skrull advancing. "This guy is *really* getting on my nerves," the Hulk growled.

"Now you know why he's so popular back home," Whitmore said sarcastically.

Turning his gaze to the sky above the warrior, the Hulk smiled grimly as he spotted Spider-Man preparing to attack. The jade giant turned back to Betty and

Whitmore. "All right, I've had my fill of this jerk for one evening. Get out of here. Find a better place to hide and stay there until the fireworks are over."

"Be careful, Bruce," said Betty. "Don't do anything reckless."

"Hey," replied the Hulk, showing his winningest smile, "it's *me*." Standing up, he turned to face the Super-Skrull.

"I know," muttered Betty as she and Whitmore headed for cover. "That's what concerns me."

K'lrt came to a halt as the Hulk turned to face him. Hidden by the green behemoth's massive frame, Betty and Whitmore scrambled over the scattered debris and out of sight.

The Super-Skrull flashed a fearsome grin at the Hulk. "You have failed, Hulk. The traitor to the Empire is dead, and so is your woman." He chuckled softly. "I imagine the grief must be overwhelming."

"No, but I've got one heck of a case of heartburn," the Hulk replied gruffly. "Listening to braggarts like you always gives me gas."

"I see," said the Super-Skrull, nodding his head as though in understanding. "You try to conceal your pain with a poor attempt at humor."

"Hey, that's *my* department!" said a voice behind the Skrull. K'lrt turned in time to see Spider-Man's red-colored soles coming at him a moment before they connected with his jaw. The impact snapped K'lrt's head back and knocked him off-balance.

"Your turn, Doc!" yelled Spider-Man.

Moving quickly, the Hulk stepped forward and delivered a devastating uppercut that floored the Super-

Skrull. Blood spurted from the warrior's mouth, and he spat out a broken tooth.

The Hulk grabbed K'lrt by the front of his uniform and pulled him close to his face. The green behemoth's eyes flashed with unbridled hatred. "I know what you're thinking, Skrull—Spider-Man and I might defeat you today, but, sooner or later, you'll be back to haunt us. That's how it's always been with people like you—no matter how many times we beat you, no matter how often we ruin your plans, *you keep coming back.*"

The Hulk's lips curled back and he sneered at K'lrt. "Well, no more! You tried to kill my wife! *My wife!* Do you think I'm going to give a punk like you an opportunity to try it again?" He violently shook his enemy like a rag doll, but K'lrt made no reply. "It's about time someone made sure you'll never hurt any more innocents," said the Hulk. "And mister, I'm just the guy to do it!"

With a roar, the Hulk began raining blow upon blow to the Skrull's face. Too stunned by the savage attack to activate any of his Fantastic Four powers, K'lrt could only make a feeble effort to defend himself.

Spider-Man was shocked by the Hulk's change in attitude. "Doc! Doc, stop!" he cried. "You're killing him!" He fired both web-shooters, catching the Hulk's fist as it rose to deliver another punch. Ignoring the pain that threatened to overwhelm him, the wall-crawler pulled as hard as his injured back would allow. Trying to stop the Hulk from throwing a punch was like using a piece of string to stop a jet fighter from taking off.

"Let him go, Doc!" yelled Spider-Man. Black spots

danced in front of his eyes—he was starting to lose consciousness. But the red-and-blue-clad hero willed himself to hang onto the taut line.

The Hulk reeled around to face Spider-Man. The web-slinger gasped, his eyes widening in surprise behind his mask as he saw the expression on the Hulk's face. It wasn't the look of a gentle giant who, just hours before, had been joking with friends. This was the face of a savage beast overcome with bloodlust.

"Oh, boy," muttered Spider-Man. "I know *that* look."

"Back off, Spider-Man!" roared the jade giant. With a powerful tug, he snapped the web-line and turned back to his prey. "I'm putting this punk out of my misery!"

Spider-Man leaped onto the Hulk's back, grabbing the giant's wrist with both hands. "Snap out of it, Doc!" he pleaded. "I'm not gonna let you kill the Skrull, no matter what he's done!"

The Hulk snapped his arm back, tossing Spider-Man a dozen feet away. The green behemoth turned his attention back to the Super-Skrull.

K'lrt's face looked like raw meat that had been pounded with a mallet. Barely conscious, he hung limply in the Hulk's grip. "N-no . . ." he muttered through a broken jaw. "Can't . . . fail again . . ."

The Hulk drew back his fist, prepared to deliver the last, fatal strike.

"No, Bruce!" cried Betty. She and Whitmore ran across the battlefield. "Let him go!"

Spider-Man leaped in front of her and put up a warning hand. "Stay back, Betty—the doc's lost it!"

Seeing his wife approach, the Hulk lowered his fist and looked quizzically at her. "Betty . . . ?"

"Yes, Bruce." Betty gestured toward the Super-Skrull. "Let him go," she said gently.

The Hulk looked at the Skrull. The jade giant's eyes widened in horror as he gazed at the damage he'd inflicted on the warrior. He opened his hand and let the alien drop, unconscious, onto the pavement.

Betty looked to Spider-Man. "It's all right," she said. The web-slinger stepped aside to let her join her husband.

"Betty, I-I'm . . . I'm sorry," the Hulk stammered. "I-I didn't mean to lose control like that . . ."

Betty gently smiled at the Hulk. "It's okay, Bruce. I understand."

Whitmore stepped up beside Spider-Man. They watched as Betty threw her arms around the Hulk's neck and the couple embraced.

Spider-Man let out a sigh of relief.

"You said a mouthful," commented Whitmore.

Spider-Man looked at the author, finally commenting on Whitmore's dramatic new appearance. "Is that a new look for you?" he asked. "No offense, but I really hate it."

"So says the fashion victim," Whitmore said drily.

Before Spider-Man could make a witty comeback, he stopped in mid-thought as his spider-sense suddenly jangled a warning!

"Doc! Hey, Doc!" he called to the Hulk. "I don't think we're out of this yet!"

The air filled with a deep, teeth-rattling rumble. The sound increased in volume until Spider-Man thought his head was going to explode. The web-slinger looked up, trying to find the source of the disturbance.

The sky above the street seemed to waver, like a

This was the face of a savage beast overcome with bloodlust.

television picture out of focus. The stars shimmered, then disappeared as a circular object—one roughly the size of three city blocks—appeared. Its hull bristled with weaponry.

"A Skrull warship," observed Whitmore. "I see they've made improvements to the cloaking device."

Spider-Man sighed. "They wouldn't be here to surrender, would they?"

"Not very likely," said Whitmore. "They're probably here to finish the job that K'lrt screwed up."

"That's what I figured you'd say," said Spider-Man. He turned to the Hulk. "You ready, Doc?"

The Hulk nodded. "Let's get this over with."

Suddenly, a beam of bright blue light stabbed down from an opening in the ship's belly. The light washed over the unconscious Super-Skrull and pulled him into the air. Within seconds, he was drawn into the craft. The opening irised close.

Spider-Man looked to Whitmore. "Tractor beam," said the author nonchalantly.

"So, what happens next?" asked Spider-Man.

As if in response to the question, the warship rose higher into the sky. With a roar of engines, it turned and soared toward the stars.

Spider-Man watched the ship fade into the distance just as the first rays of sunlight were creeping over the New York skyline. The battle was over, and they had all survived.

The wall-crawler scratched his head and turned to face the Banners and Whitmore. He jerked a thumb in the direction of the warship.

"Well," commented Spider-Man, "*that* was certainly anti-climactic."

CHAPTER
10

"**H**ow's that feel?" asked the emergency room doctor as she applied a salve to Spider-Man's back.

"Muuuch better," sighed the web-slinger. He sat on the edge of an examining table, his legs dangling over one side. Spidey tapped his heels against the table in a steady rhythm, and drummed his fingers on the padded cushion on which he sat. For a grown man, he was acting far too much like a kid impatiently waiting for his mother to let him go out and play.

Rolling his head around in small circles, Spider-Man worked to loosen his stiff neck muscles. He smiled contentedly as he felt his vertebrae click back into place.

The emergency room of St. Peter's Hospital was already packed to the rafters with hordes of injured people brought in from the urban battlefield a half-mile to the west. The sound of approaching ambulance sirens was a clear sign that more victims were on their way. When Spider-Man had arrived, accompanied by the Banners and Whitmore, it had taken the doctor some time to convince him that he should receive immediate medical attention. After all, as he pointed out, there were other people in greater need of care. Spidey finally acquiesced when the Hulk threatened to sit on him so the doctor could do her work.

The doctor—whose nameplate simply read "M. Takahashi"—finished dressing Spider-Man's wounds with fresh bandages. "All right, that should do it for now," she said. "If it wasn't so apparent that your wounds already show signs of healing, I'd keep you under observation for two weeks, at least."

"And force me to eat *hospital food?*" gasped Spider-Man. He shivered. "Eww. I'd rather fight Galactus."

"Oh, it's not that bad," chided Dr. Takahashi. "As long as, you know, you avoid the stuff that moves." She smiled. "Try and stay out of trouble for a while, all right? Give your wounds the proper time to heal."

"I'll do my best, Doc."

Takahashi smiled. "Riiight." She shook the web-slinger's hand. "Well, it was nice meeting you, Spider-Man."

"Same here, Doc," replied Spidey. "Thanks for the repair job."

"Don't mention it." Takahashi turned and left the room.

"All fixed up, Spider-Man?" said a voice behind the wall-crawler.

Spider-Man turned to find Major Nefertiti Jones standing in the doorway. Still wearing her scorched battle armor, her hair neatly tied back, Jones looked the picture of cool military authority. From the signs of strain on her face, though, it was apparent to Spider-Man that she was forcing herself to remain on her feet until the crisis was completely over.

"As best as can be," said Spidey. He hopped off the examining table. "What's up, Major?"

Jones wiggled a finger in a come-with-me gesture. "Got a little problem I need your advice on."

Spider-Man followed the major down a crowded hallway to the doctors' lounge. The doorway was guarded by two of the biggest SAFE agents he'd ever seen. Both women were heavily armed and looked as deadly as their weapons. They nodded silently at Jones as she approached.

"By the way," Spidey said to Jones, "how's your second-in-command?"

"Elfman's a little scorched, and he's got a mild concussion, but he should be back on his feet in a few days." Jones voice took on a husky tone. "I wish I could say that about all the men," she said softly.

"I'm sorry, Major," said Spider-Man.

Jones cleared her throat and straightened up, becoming all-business again. "Not your fault, Spider-Man," she said curtly. "We all know the risks going in. It's part of the job."

Maybe you're right, Major, thought Spider-Man, *but it doesn't make coping with someone's death any easier.*

Jones opened the door and gestured Spider-Man inside. The walls of the lounge were painted a pale green, a color made even more nauseating in the light of flickering fluorescent bulbs. The furniture consisted of a worn leather couch, some equally worn chairs, a soda vending machine, and a television. The couch was occupied by Betty and Whitmore, with the Hulk sitting cross-legged on the floor beside them. Whitmore still looked like a Skrull. All three were engrossed in watching the TV, on which an *I Love Lucy* episode was playing. The trio laughed uproariously as the show's star, Lucille Ball, struggled to stop a conveyor belt from dumping a never-ending line of chocolate candies on the floor.

Whitmore wiped away the tears of laughter that were streaming down his face. "I love that show," he sighed.

Spider-Man gestured toward Whitmore and leaned close to Jones. "Is this what you wanted my opinion on?" he asked softly.

Jones nodded.

Betty looked up and spotted the wall-crawler. "Spider-Man! How do you feel?"

Spidey shrugged. "Well, I won't be looking to pick a fight with Doctor Octopus right away, but I'm feeling a lot better. How are you guys doing?"

"I'm doing fine," replied the Hulk. "Betty's a little bruised and sore, but nothing to really worry about . . . or so her *doctor* told me."

"Bruce . . ." Betty said in a warning tone.

"Sorry, honey," said the Hulk, "but I worry about you. *I'm* the one who usually gets highways dropped on his head."

Betty flashed him a smile. "I understand."

The Hulk waved a hand toward Whitmore. "As for Berk . . . well, as you can see, he still looks like a toad."

Whitmore glared at his green-skinned friend. "I think I liked it better when you were slow-witted and monosyllabic." He reached up to scratch the pointed tip of one oversized ear. "Besides, it's not like I haven't tried changing back since K'lrt . . . departed. It's just that, after more than forty years in one body-type, it seems my shapeshifting abilities were only good for one more change."

"It could be worse," said Spidey. "The Super-Skrull could've succeeded in his mission."

"Actually, he *did* succeed," said Whitmore. "In a way."

"How so, Berk?" asked the Hulk.

The author gestured toward his own face. "Well, just *look* at me, Bruce. The odds are good that I'll be stuck in this form for the rest of my days. Maybe you didn't notice, but I don't exactly look like the author photograph on the back of my books anymore. Besides, I'm a *Skrull*, for Pete's sake. Once word of that gets around, I'll have even more enemies after me than just the ones I've spent thirty years cultivating." Whitmore glanced at Jones. "Not to mention the hordes of government agencies that will be divided among those wanting me locked away for being a possible Skrull spy, those wanting to interrogate me to learn all they can about the Empire, and those inclined toward dissecting me to see what makes me tick."

"That brings up another question, Berk," said the Hulk. "Why are you here? Why would a Skrull officer be hiding out on Earth? And why is it so important to the Empire that he be killed?"

Whitmore paused for a moment, as though gathering his thoughts. "All right. First off, my real name is Kroton. I'm not going to give you all the details of my formative years—that kind of minutiae bores even *me*.

I'll just skip ahead to the pertinent parts of my life that lead up to last night's events."

Whitmore cleared his throat. "When I was eighteen years old, I enrolled in the Warriors' Academy, as all male Skrulls are expected to do when they come of age. I was in a class of three hundred cadets, and we were taught just one subject: the art of war.

"After six years at the academy, I graduated in the top percentile of my class and quickly rose through the ranks. By the age of thirty, I was first officer on a warship, often leading landing parties on unexplored worlds. On more than one occasion my men and I had to fight our way out of some pretty hostile situations. By fifty—still a kid by Skrull standards—I was commanding a small outpost on Krylos. But a series of attacks on other outposts suddenly put all worlds in the Empire on alert. The Kree—who hadn't been heard from for the last century—decided the universe had become too quiet. They wanted a fight, and Emperor Dorrek was only too happy to meet the challenge.

"The war had been raging for six years when I received new orders from the Imperial Throneworld. My next stop was Kallusa, a planet on the Kree-Skrull border, where a prisoner of war camp had been built. I was to be camp commandant.

"When I arrived on Kallusa, I decided a tour of the camp was in order before I settled in to my new duties. More than that, I wanted to see what the 'mighty' Kree looked like up close. For centuries, the blue-skinned aliens had been warring with my people. Not a day of my life had elapsed without a reminder from my father or my superiors about the evils of the 'accursed Kree.' Now, I had an opportunity to berate those who had been foolish enough to dare oppose the great Skrull Empire! With the warriors falling in step behind us, Captain K'rlmar—my second-in-command—and I headed across the compound.

"We arrived at the first habitat—a dilapidated barracks carved from rough stone blocks with crude hand tools. Torn rags were fastened over the 'windows' from the inside—poor protection against the harsh, stinging winter gales. With a contemptuous grin on my face, I strode through the doorway, ready to laugh in the faces of my enemies . . . *and found myself facing women and children.*"

Whitmore shuddered, visibly shaken by the memory. "The women ranged in age from eighteen to one hundred, the children no older than nine or ten. Their clothing was torn and faded, their hair matted with dirt, their bright blue skin covered with filth and sores. They all looked as though they hadn't eaten in days. The smile I'd had plastered on my face quickly faded as I saw a look of absolute terror come into their eyes at the sight of me. It's a look I've spent years trying to forget . . . but the memory's never gone away."

Behind his mask, Spider-Man's eyes widened in surprise. He looked at Whitmore. "That's the opening scene of *Reality of Evil.*"

Whitmore nodded. "The book had nothing to do with World War II, and everything to do with my year at the camp. It was my way of dealing with the ghosts of my past."

"So what did you do, Berk?" asked Betty.

"I immediately began instituting changes to improve the prisoners' living conditions," Whitmore replied. "After a year, word finally reached the Emperor about my 'leisure camp' for Kree prisoners. He wasn't exactly pleased with the news, and ordered my death. I fled Kallusa just as a Skrull warship dropped into orbit around the planet. I drifted from world to world for ten or twelve years, then arrived in New York in the late 1940s. I spent days studying copies of reports on Earth culture that had been filed by Skrull spies over the course of centuries. Then, after assuming a human appearance, I hit the libraries, reading everything I could get my hands on—novels, plays, poetry. I overloaded on culture."

"But what got you interested in human rights issues on Earth?" asked Spider-Man.

"Well," said Whitmore, "I hadn't planned on getting involved with problems on this planet—I was just in need of a place to hide out from the Empire. But imagine my shock when I learned from my research at the libraries that humans could be just as vile as my own people. The horrors of World War II, minorities being treated as second-class citizens, people around the world being punished for their beliefs in a fair system of government—it was the Kree-Skrull hatred all over again. I swore I wouldn't allow another Kallusa to happen."

Whitmore smiled. "A pretty lofty ambition, huh? Well, it's been a long road toward peace, but I'm happy to see that things are beginning to change on this little mudball. It's still a long way from perfect, but in time . . ." He paused. "And it seems that my efforts have had more of a far-reaching effect than I could have imagined." He looked at Betty. "Remember all those hypothetical people out in the universe you had been talking about? The ones who might be carrying a similar message of equal rights for all races? *They exist.* In fact, I've been in contact over the last decade with some of the leaders of a human rights movement on Kallusa. My message has been spreading like wildfire. That's why K'lrt was sent to kill me—to shut me up before the worlds ruled by the Empire rebel and fight for their freedom. Too bad for the Empress that she sent the wrong man for the job."

"So what happens now?" asked the Hulk.

Whitmore nodded toward Jones. "Well, I think that's up to the good Major here. She's got two choices: Let me go, or turn me over to some clandestine organization that deals with aliens, like you see on *The X-Files.*"

"But where would you go, Berk?" asked Betty. "It's more than likely that the Empress will send more killers after you, no matter where you go. At least here you've got friends willing to protect you."

"Like I said before, Betty," said Whitmore, "I'm not comfortable with people fighting my battles for me. I appreciate the concern, but I'm a big boy. Besides, if the Empress is so worried about my human rights message getting around, then I think it's time I became more active in its spread . . . by traveling back to the Empire." He waved his hands to quiet Betty's protest. "I know, I know—it's like sticking my head in the lion's mouth. But the possible outcome for change would be worth the risk." Whitmore affectionately patted Betty's hand. "It's something I *have* to do."

Betty smiled. "All right, Berk. I understand."

Whitmore turned to face Jones. "What's it gonna be, Major?"

Jones stood quietly, looking at the Banners and Spider-

Man, then back to Whitmore. "My team is going to make a sweep of the hospital," she finally said, "just to make sure there are no Skrull spies lurking around. I expect to be back here in ten minutes."

Spider-Man nodded. "Understood, Major. And thanks."

Jones turned on her heel and opened the door to leave. She paused in the frame and turned back to Whitmore. "I've never been a fan of yours, Mr. Whitmore, but I've always admired your politics. I wanted you to know that I appreciate all the fighting you've done to try and make a change." She paused. "Thank you."

Whitmore looked stunned. "Thank *you*, Major," he replied.

Jones nodded and closed the door behind her as she left.

The Hulk unfolded his legs and stood up. "And that's our cue to book out of here." He turned to Spider-Man. "Thanks for the assist, bug-man. But let's try and keep out of each other's way in the future, all right?"

"No problem, Doc," said Spidey. "Just keep the property damage to a minimum and we should get along fine."

Whitmore turned to Spider-Man and extended his hand. "Thanks for all your help, Spider-Man. You're a man with terrible taste in clothing, but you make one heck of a warrior in your own right. I'm glad we met."

Spider-Man shook Whitmore's hand. "So am I. I really hope you're able to succeed in changing people's minds."

"*Thanks for all your help, Spider-Man. You're a man with terrible taste in clothing, but you make one heck of a warrior . . .*"

"Well, it won't be easy," Whitmore admitted, "but I've already got a human rights case in mind that should shake up the Empire when I go public with it. Someone who's gonna need a great deal of help in getting released from a Skrull detention camp."

"Who do you have in mind?" asked Spidey.

Whitmore smiled broadly. "Why, the Super-Skrull, of course. The guy might be an ineffectual idiot, but even he has a right to humane treatment. If I can get him released, the Empress is gonna have a lot to worry about."

Spidey shook his head in disbelief. "You're amazing."

"I've been saying that for years," chuckled Whitmore. "Nice to see that people have gotten *that* message."

The Hulk opened the door and looked into the corridor. "Time to go, Berk." Betty followed the jade giant out of the room, pausing only long enough to say a quick "thank you" to Spidey.

Whitmore smiled at Spider-Man. "Take care of yourself, web-head. I hope we'll get to meet again under better circumstances. Maybe next time we can discuss how my wisdom influenced you in finding a new costume designer." With a wink of an eye, Whitmore turned and, laughing, left the room, closing the door behind him.

Spider-Man chuckled softly for a moment, then sighed and lowered himself onto the couch. Fatigue was creeping over him, and he needed to relax.

Spider-Man thought about the risks Whitmore was facing. One man was going to go up against a galactic empire, face down his enemies, and try to change them for the better. But could one man—even a Berkley Whitmore—make such a change to the vast Skrull Empire?

"You know," Spidey said to himself as he drifted off to sleep, "I wouldn't be surprised if he actually succeeded. . . ."

THE END

ARCHWAY PAPERBACKS SPIDER-MAN® SWEEPSTAKES

Official Rules:

1. No Purchase Necessary. Enter by submitting the completed Official Entry Form or by sending on a 3" x 5" card on which you have written your name, address, and a daytime telephone number to the Spider-Man Sweepstakes, 1230 Sixth Ave., 13th floor, New York, NY 10020. Entries must be received by 12/31/97. Not responsible for postage due, lost, late, illegible, stolen, incomplete, mutilated or misdirected mail. Enter as often as you wish, but one entry per envelope. 500 winners will be selected at random from all eligible entries received in a drawing to be held on or about 12/31/97.

2. Prizes: 500 Spider-Man: The Sinister Six CD-ROMs (approximate retail value: $39.95 each).

3. The sweepstakes is open to legal residents of the U.S. and Canada (except Quebec). Prizes will be awarded to a winner's parent or legal guardian if winner is under 18. Void in Puerto Rico and wherever prohibited by law. Employees, their immediate family members and others living in their household of Simon & Schuster, Inc., Viacom International, Inc., Byron Preiss Multimedia Company, Inc., and Marvel Entertainment Group, Inc. and their respective suppliers, affiliates, divisions, and agencies are not eligible. Prizes are not transferable and may not be substituted except by sponsor for reason of unavailability in which case a prize of equal or greater value will be awarded. One prize per household. The odds of winning a prize depend upon the number of eligible entries received. All prizes will be awarded.

4. If a winner is a Canadian resident, then he/she must correctly answer a time-limited, skill-based question administered by mail.

5. By participating, entrants agree to these rules and decisions of the judges which are final in all respects. Each winner may be required to execute and return an affidavit of eligibility and publicity/liability release within 15 days of notification attempt or an alternative winner may be selected.

6. Simon & Schuster, Inc., Viacom International, Inc., Byron Preiss Multimedia Company, Inc., and Marvel Entertainment Group, Inc. shall have no liability for any injury, loss, or damage of any kind, including without limitation, property damage, personal injury and/or death, arising out of any participation in this sweepstakes or acceptance or use of the prize.

7. All expenses on the receipt and use of the prize, and all federal, state and local taxes are the responsibility of the winners. Winners will be notified by mail. By accepting a prize, winners grant Archway Paperbacks the right to use their names, likenesses, and entries for any advertising, promotion and publicity purposes without further compensation or permission, except where prohibited by law. For a list of prize winners (available after 12/31/97) send a stamped, self-addressed envelope by 1/31/98, to Prize Winners, Archway Paperbacks/Spider-Man Sweepstakes, 13th Floor, 1230 Avenue of the Americas, NY, NY 10020.